PENGUIN POPULAR CLASSICS

THE TEMPEST
BY WILLIAM SHAKESPEARE

PENGUIN POPULAR CLASSICS

THE TEMPEST

WILLIAM SHAKESPEARE

PENGUIN BOOKS
A PENGUIN/GODFREY CAVE EDITION

PENGUIN BOOKS

Published by the Penguin Group
Penguin Books Ltd, 27 Wrights Lane, London w8 5tz, England
Penguin Books USA Inc., 375 Hudson Street, New York, New York 10014, USA
Penguin Books Australia Ltd, Ringwood, Victoria, Australia
Penguin Books Canada Ltd, 10 Alcorn Avenue, Toronto, Ontario, Canada m4v 3b2
Penguin Books (NZ) Ltd, 182–190 Wairau Road, Auckland 10, New Zealand

Penguin Books Ltd, Registered Offices: Harmondsworth, Middlesex, England

Published in Penguin Popular Classics 1994
1 3 5 7 9 10 8 6 4 2

Printed in England by Clays Ltd, St Ives plc

CONTENTS

THE WORKS OF SHAKESPEARE

PLAYS

WILLIAM SHAKESPEARE

William Shakespeare was born at Stratford upon Avon in April, 1564. He was the third child, and eldest son, of John Shakespeare and Mary Arden. His father was one of the most prosperous men of Stratford who held in turn the chief offices in the town. His mother was of gentle birth, the daughter of Robert Arden of Wilmcote. In December, 1582, Shakespeare married Ann Hathaway, daughter of a farmer of Shottery, near Stratford; their first child Susanna was baptized on May 6, 1583, and twins, Hamnet and Judith, on February 22, 1585. Little is known of Shakespeare's early life; but it is unlikely that a writer who dramatized such an incomparable range and variety of human kinds and experiences should have spent his early manhood entirely in placid pursuits in a country town. There is one tradition, not universally accepted, that he fled from Stratford because he was in trouble for deer stealing, and had fallen foul of Sir Thomas Lucy, the local magnate; another that he was for some time a schoolmaster.

From 1592 onwards the records are much fuller. In March, 1592, the Lord Strange's players produced a new play at the Rose Theatre called *Harry the Sixth*, which was very successful, and was probably the *First Part of Henry VI*. In the autumn of 1592 Robert Greene, the best known of the professional writers, as he was dying wrote a letter to three fellow writers in which he warned them against the ingratitude of players in general, and in particular against an 'upstart crow' who 'supposes he is as much able to bombast out a blank verse as the best of you: and being an absolute Johannes Factotum is in his own conceit the only

7

Shake-scene in a country.' This is the first reference to Shakespeare, and the whole passage suggests that Shakespeare had become suddenly famous as a playwright. At this time Shakespeare was brought into touch with Edward Alleyne the great tragedian, and Christopher Marlowe, whose thundering parts of Tamburlaine, the Jew of Malta and Dr Faustus Alleyne was acting, as well as Hieronimo, the hero of Kyd's *Spanish Tragedy*, the most famous of all Elizabethan plays.

In April, 1593, Shakespeare published his poem *Venus and Adonis*, which was dedicated to the young Earl of Southampton: it was a great and lasting success, and was reprinted nine times in the next few years. In May, 1594, his second poem, *The Rape of Lucrece*, was also dedicated to Southampton.

There was little playing in 1593, for the theatres were shut during a severe outbreak of the plague; but in the autumn of 1594, when the plague ceased, the playing companies were re-organized, and Shakespeare became a sharer in the Lord Chamberlain's company who went to play in the Theatre in Shoreditch. During these months Marlowe and Kyd had died. Shakespeare was thus for a time without a rival. He had already written the three parts of *Henry VI*, *Richard III*, *Titus Andronicus*, *Two Gentlemen of Verona*, *Love's Labour's Lost*, *The Comedy of Errors*, and *The Taming of the Shrew*. Soon afterwards he wrote the first of his greater plays – *Romeo and Juliet* – and he followed this success in the next three years with *A Midsummer Night's Dream*, *Richard II*, and *The Merchant of Venice*. The two parts of *Henry IV*, introducing Falstaff, the most popular of all his comic characters, were written in 1597-8.

The company left the Theatre in 1597 owing to disputes over a renewal of the ground lease, and went to play at the

Curtain in the same neighbourhood. The disputes continued throughout 1598, and at Christmas the players settled the matter by demolishing the old Theatre and re-erecting a new playhouse on the South bank of the Thames, near Southwark Cathedral. This playhouse was named the Globe. The expenses of the new building were shared by the chief members of the Company, including Shakespeare, who was now a man of some means. In 1596 he had bought New Place, a large house in the centre of Stratford, for £60, and through his father purchased a coat-of-arms from the Heralds, which was the official recognition that he and his family were gentlefolk.

By the summer of 1598 Shakespeare was recognized as the greatest of English dramatists. Booksellers were printing his more popular plays, at times even in pirated or stolen version, and he received a remarkable tribute from a young writer named Francis Meres, in his book *Palladis Tamia*. In a long catalogue of English authors Meres gave Shakespeare more prominence than any other writer, and mentioned by name twelve of his plays.

Shortly before the Globe was opened, Shakespeare had completed the cycle of plays dealing with the whole story of the Wars of the Roses with *Henry V*. It was followed by *As You Like it*, and *Julius Caesar*, the first of the maturer tragedies. In the next three years he wrote *Troilus and Cressida*, *The Merry Wives of Windsor*, *Hamlet* and *Twelfth Night*.

On March 24, 1603, Queen Elizabeth died. The company had often performed before her, but they found her successor a far more enthusiastic patron. One of the first acts of King James was to take over the company and to promote them to be his own servants, so that henceforward they were known as the King's Men. They acted now very frequently at Court, and prospered accordingly. In the early years of the reign Shakespeare wrote the more sombre comedies, *All's Well that Ends Well*, and *Measure for Measure*, which were followed by *Othello*, *Macbeth*, and *King Lear*. Then he returned to Roman themes with *Antony and Cleopatra* and *Coriolanus*.

Since 1601 Shakespeare had been writing less, and there were now a number of rival dramatists who were introducing new styles of drama, particularly Ben Jonson (whose first successful comedy, *Every Man in his Humour*, was acted by Shakespeare's company in 1598), Chapman, Dekker, Marston, and Beaumont and Fletcher who began to write in 1607. In 1608 the King's Men acquired a second playhouse, an indoor private theatre in the fashionable quarter of the Blackfriars. At private theatres, plays were performed indoors; the prices charged were higher than in the public playhouses, and the audience consequently was more select. Shakespeare seems to have retired from the stage about this time: his name does not occur in the various lists of players after 1607. Henceforward he lived for the most part at Stratford, where he was regarded as one of the most important citizens. He still wrote a few plays, and he tried his hand at the new form of tragi-comedy – a play with tragic incidents but a happy ending – which Beaumont and Fletcher had popularized. He wrote four of these – *Pericles*, *Cymbeline*, *The Winter's Tale*, and *The Tempest*, which was acted at Court in 1611. For the last four years of his life he lived in retirement. His son Hamnet had died in 1596: his two daughters were now married. Shakespeare died at Stratford upon Avon on April 23, 1616, and was buried in the chancel of the church, before the high altar. Shortly afterwards a memorial which still exists, with a portrait bust, was set up on the North wall. His wife survived him.

When Shakespeare died fourteen of his plays had been separately published in Quarto booklets. In 1623 his surviving fellow actors, John Heming and Henry Condell, with the co-operation of a number of printers, published a collected edition of thirty-six plays in one Folio volume, with an engraved portrait, memorial verses by Ben Jonson and others, and an Epistle to the Reader in which Heming and Condell make the interesting note that Shakespeare's 'hand and mind went together, and what he thought, he uttered with that easiness that we have scarce received from him a blot in his papers.'

The plays as printed in the Quartos or the Folio differ considerably from the usual modern text. They are often not divided into scenes, and sometimes not even into acts. Nor are there place-headings at the beginning of each scene, because in the Elizabethan theatre there was no scenery. They are carelessly printed and the spelling is erratic.

THE ELIZABETHAN THEATRE

Although plays of one sort and another had been acted for many generations, no permanent playhouse was erected in England until 1576. In the 1570's the Lord Mayor and Aldermen of the City of London and the players were constantly at variance. As a result James Burbage, then the leader of the great Earl of Leicester's players, decided that he would erect a playhouse outside the jurisdiction of the Lord Mayor, where the players would no longer be hindered by the authorities. Accordingly in 1576 he built the Theatre in Shoreditch, at that time a suburb of London. The experiment was successful, and by 1592 there were two more playhouses in London, the Curtain (also in Shoreditch, and the Rose on the south bank of the river, near Southwark Cathedral.

Elizabethan players were accustomed to act on a variety of stages; in the great hall of a nobleman's house, or one of the Queen's palaces, in town halls and in yards, as well as their own theatre.

The public playhouse for which most of Shakespeare's plays were written was a small and intimate affair. The outside measurement of the Fortune Theatre, which was built in 1600 to rival the new Globe, was but eighty feet square. Playhouses were usually circular or octagonal, with three tiers of galleries looking down upon the yard or pit, which was open to the sky. The stage jutted out into the yard so that the actors came forward into the midst of their audience.

Over the stage there was a roof, and on either side doors by which the characters entered or disappeared. Over the back of the stage ran a gallery or upper stage which was used whenever an upper scene was needed, as when Romeo climbs up to Juliet's bedroom, or the citizens of Angiers address King John from the walls. The space beneath this upper stage was known as the tiring house; it was concealed from the audience by a curtain which would be drawn back to reveal an inner stage, for such scenes as the witches' cave in Macbeth, Prospero's cell or Juliet's tomb.

There was no general curtain concealing the whole stage, so that all scenes on the main stage began with an entrance and ended with an exit. Thus in tragedies the dead must be carried away. There was no scenery, and therefore no limit to the number of scenes, for a scene came to an end when the characters left the stage. When it was necessary for the exact locality of a scene to be known, then Shakespeare

THE GLOBE THEATRE

Wood-engraving by R. J. Beedham after a reconstruction by J. C. Adams

indicated it in the dialogue; otherwise a simple property or a garment was sufficient; a chair or stool showed an indoor scene, a man wearing riding boots was a messenger, a king wearing armour was on the battlefield, or the like. Such simplicity was on the whole an advantage; the spectator was not distracted by the setting and Shakespeare was able to use as many scenes as he wished. The action passed by very quickly: a play of 2500 lines of verse could be acted in two hours. Moreover, since the actor was so close to his audience, the slightest subtlety of voice and gesture was easily appreciated.

The company was a 'Fellowship of Players', who were all partners and sharers. There were usually ten to fifteen full members, with three or four boys, and some paid servants. Shakespeare had therefore to write for his team. The chief actor in the company was Richard Burbage, who first distinguished himself as Richard III; for him Shakespeare wrote his great tragic parts. An important member of the company was the clown or low comedian. From 1594 to 1600 the company's clown was Will Kemp; he was succeeded by Robert Armin. No women were allowed to appear on the stage, and all women's parts were taken by boys.

THE TEMPEST

The Tempest was one of the last of Shakespeare's plays. It was written about 1611. There is a record in the *Revels Accounts* of payment for plays acted at Court in that year which includes a note that on 'Hallowmas Night (1st November) was presented at Whitehall before the King's Majesty a play called The Tempest', by the King's Players. *The Tempest* was again played at Whitehall as one of fourteen plays acted during the elaborate festivities at the marriage of the Princess Elizabeth to the Elector Palatine in February, 1613.

No direct or obvious source for the story has been found. A German play, called *Comedia von der schonen Sidea*, written by Jacob Ayrer, of Nuremberg, before 1605 has some resemblances: it tells of a magician Prince who has a spirit attendant, and an only daughter who falls in love with the son of her father's enemy. If there is a connection between this play and *The Tempest*, it is probable that both drew from some common original in an older English play, for several of Ayrer's plays were adapted from plays taken over to Germany by English players. But stories of magicians with only daughters are common stock for fairy tales.

The story of the wreck and the mysterious island owes a good deal to an event which was recent and sensational. It can best be summarized in the words of Stow's *Annals*, as continued by Edmund Howes:

'In the year 1609 the Adventurers and Company of Virginia sent from London, a fleet of eight ships with people to supply and make strong the Colony in Virginia, Sir

Thomas Gates being General in a ship of 300 ton. In this ship was also Sir George Somers, who was Admiral, and Captain Newport vice-Admiral, and with them about 160 persons; this ship was Admiral, and kept company with the rest of the fleet to the height of 30 degrees, and being then assembled to consult touching divers matters, they were surprised with a most extreme violent storm which scattered the whole fleet yet all the rest of the fleet bent their course for Virginia, where by God's special favour they arrived safely but this great ship, though new, and far stronger than any of the rest fell into a great leak, so as mariners and passengers were forced for three days' space to do their utmost to save themselves from sudden sinking: but notwithstanding their incessant pumping, and casting out of water by buckets, and all other means, yet the water covered all the goods, within the hold, and all men were utterly tired and spent in strength, and overcome with labour, and hopeless of any succour, most of them were gone to sleep, yielding themselves to the mercy of the sea, being all very desirous to die upon any shore wheresoever. Sir George Somers sitting at the stern, seeing the ship desperate of relief, looking every minute when the ship would sink, he espied land, which according to his, and Captain Newport's opinion, they judged it should be that dreadful coast of the Bermodes, which islands were of all nations said and supposed to be enchanted and inhabited with witches and devils, which grew by reason of accustomed monstrous thunder, storm, and tempest, near unto those Islands, also for that the whole coast is so wondrous dangerous of rocks, that few can approach them, but with unspeakable hazard of shipwrack. Sir George Somers, Sir Thomas Gates, Captain Newport, and the rest, suddenly agreed of two evils to choose the least, and so in a kind of desperate resolution, directed the ship mainly for these Islands; which by God's divine providence at a high water ran right between two strong rocks, where it stuck fast without breaking. Which gave leisure and good opportunity for them to hoist out their boat, and to land all their people as well as sailors, soldiers, and others in good safety, and being come ashore, they were soon refreshed and cheered, the soil and air being most sweet and delicate. The salt water did great spoil to most of the ship's lading and victual, yet some meal was well recovered, with many particular things for their common use, and they all humbly thanked God for His great mercy in so preserving them from destruction.

'Then presently they sought farther into the Island for food, which being never yet inhabited by any people, was overgrown with woods, and the woods replenished with wild swine; which swine as it is very probable swam thither out of some shipwrack. They found also great multitude of fowl of sundry kinds, being then in a manner very tame; they found some fruit, as mulberries, pears, and palmytoes, with stately cedar-trees; and in the sea, and in the rocks, great plenty of most pleasant and wholesome fish.

'Here of necessity they were constrained to stay almost ten months, in which space by the special Mercy, and Divine Providence of Almighty God, to make good the discovery of the Islands unto them, that they by diligence and industry saved so much of the timber, tackling and other things out of their great ship which lay wracked, and stuck fast between two rocks, as therewithal, and with such supply of stuff as they found in those Islands, they builded their two vessels, the lesser whereof so soon as it was finished, it was manned, and sent to go to the Colony in Virginia. to signify unto them how all things had happened with their commanders and their company, and that they would shortly set sail for Virginia, and when the bigger vessel was finished, and victualled with swine's flesh, and with what else that place would afford them, these Commanders, with all their company embarked themselves, and by God's great Mercy, arrived safely at Virginia, when all Englishmen deemed them to be utterly cast away.'

News of these events reached England in the early autumn of 1610, and two pamphlets were printed – 'A discovery of the Barmudas' and 'A Declaration of the Estate of the Colony in Virginia'. About a year later William Strachey, who was one of those cast ashore on the Bermudas, wrote a 'True Reportory of the Wreck and Redemption of Sir Thomas Gates upon and from the Islands of the Bermudas'. This was not printed until 1625, but as a number of phrases in Strachey's report seem to have been caught up into *The Tempest*, it is possible that Shakespeare saw it in manuscript.

Prospero's Island is not, however, situated in the West Indies, but in the Mediterranean, somewhere off the direct course between Tunis and Naples. Shakespeare's idea of the magic island may also have been first suggested by a passage in William Parry's *New and Large Discourse of the Travels of Sir Anthony Shirley, Knight*, describing Shirley's astonishing journeyings in Persia and Russia. This book came out in 1601, and Shakespeare seems to have read it, for he refers more than once to Shirley's Persian adventure. Parry describes how 'within two days' passage of Candia [Crete], as we came towards Ciprus (which I had almost omitted) there is also a Greekish isle (whose name – I am ashamed therefore – I have quite forgotten), whereupon we touched and watered, which is some half-mile over, having one religious house therein and alone, with about some twenty Greek friggots [friars] inhabiting the same, which is (as we thought) another Eden; and the most pleasant place that ever our eyes beheld, for the exercise of a solitary and contemplative life: for it is furnished with the foison of all God's good blessings. All kinds of fruits (as apples, pears, plums, oranges, lemons, pomegranates, and the like) in great abundance groweth there: with most pleasant gardens, replenished with all manner of odoriferous flowers and wholesome herbs for sallets and medicines: wherein breaketh forth many fresh and crystal clear springs of water: having therewithal cattle (as beeves and muttons there naturally bred) more than sufficient to serve that house. In our travels many times, falling into dangers and unpleasant places, this only island would be the place where we would wish ourselves to end our lives.' [*Anthony Sherley: his Persian Adventure*, by Sir E. Denison Ross, p. 105.]

Another book, which Shakespeare obviously read when writing *The Tempest*, was John Florio's translation of Montaigne's *Essays*, published in 1603; for a passage from the Essay 'Of the Cannibals' (No. XXX) is followed very closely in Gonzalo's little discourse of his ideal commonwealth [p. 49, l. 16]. Montaigne notes how one of his servants told him of a tribe of savages which followed the rule of nature, 'it is a nation, would I answer Plato, that hath no kind of traffic, no knowledge of Letters, no intelligence of numbers, no name of magistrate, nor of politic superiority; no use of service, of riches or of poverty; no contracts, no successions, no partitions, no occupation but idle; no respect of kindred, but common, no apparel but natural, no manuring of lands, no use of wine, corn, or metal. The very words that import lying, falsehood, treason, dissimulations, covetousness, envy, detraction, and pardon, were never heard of amongst them. How dissonant would he find his imaginary commonwealth from this perfection?' Shakespeare, however, had a less idealistic notion of the savage; Caliban's vocabulary is richer and more lurid.

The Tempest was not published until the Folio in 1623, wherein it is printed first. The text was unusually well prepared for the press; it was divided into Acts and Scenes, the stage directions are very full and interesting, and the punctuation is excellent.

The present text follows the Folio very closely. Spelling has been modernized, but the original arrangement and the punctuation (which 'points' the text for reading aloud) has been kept, except in a few places where it seemed obviously wrong. The reader who is used to an accepted text may thus find some unfamiliarities, but the text itself is nearer to that used by Shakespeare's own company.

The Tempest

THE SCENE: AN UNINHABITED ISLAND

—

THE ACTORS' NAMES

ALONSO, King of Naples
SEBASTIAN, his brother
PROSPERO, the right Duke of Milan
ANTHONIO, his brother, the usurping Duke of Milan
FERDINAND, son to the King of Naples
GONZALO, an honest old Councillor
ADRIAN,
FRANCISCO, } Lords
CALIBAN, a salvage and deformed Slave
TRINCULO, a Jester
STEPHANO, a drunken Butler
Master of a Ship
Boatswain
Mariners
MIRANDA, daughter to Prospero
ARIEL, an airy Spirit
IRIS,
CERES,
JUNO, } Spirits
Nymphs,
Reapers

I. 1

*A tempestuous noise of thunder and lightning heard:
enter a Ship-master, and a Boatswain.*

MASTER: Boatswain.

BOATSWAIN: Here Master: what cheer?

MASTER: Good: speak to th' mariners: fall to't, yarely, or
we run ourselves aground, bestir, bestir.

Exit.

Enter Mariners.

BOATSWAIN: Heigh my hearts, cheerly, cheerly my
hearts: yare, yare: take in the top sail: tend to th'
Master's whistle: blow till thou burst thy wind, if room
enough.

*Enter Alonso, Sebastian, Anthonio, Ferdinand, Gonzalo,
and others.*

ALONSO: Good Boatswain have care: where's the Master?
Play the men.

BOATSWAIN: I pray now keep below.

ANTHONIO: Where is the Master. Boatswain?

BOATSWAIN: Do you not hear him? You mar our labour,
keep your cabins; you do assist the storm.

GONZALO: Nay, good be patient.

BOATSWAIN: When the sea is: hence, what cares these
roarers for the name of King? To cabin; silence: trouble
us not.

GONZALO: Good, yet remember whom thou hast aboard.

BOATSWAIN: None that I more love than myself. You are
a Councillor, if you can command these elements to
silence, and work the peace of the present, we will not
hand a rope more, use your authority: if you cannot

give thanks you have liv'd so long, and make yourself
ready in your cabin for the mischance of the hour, if it
so hap. Cheerly good hearts: out of our way I say.

Exit.

GONZALO: I have great comfort from this fellow: methinks he hath no drowning mark upon him, his com-
plexion is perfect gallows: stand fast good Fate to his
hanging, make the rope of his destiny our cable. for our
own doth little advantage: if he be not born to be
hang'd, our case is miserable.

Exeunt.

Enter Boatswain.

BOATSWAIN: Down with the topmast: yare, lower, lower, bring her to try with main course. A plague——

A cry within. Enter Sebastian, Anthonio, and Gonzalo.

upon this howling: they are louder than the weather,
or our office: yet again? what do you here? Shall we
give o'er and drown, have you a mind to sink?

SEBASTIAN: A pox o' your throat, you bawling, blasphe-
mous incharitable dog.

BOATSWAIN: Work you then.

ANTHONIO: Hang cur, hang, you whoreson, insolent noise-
maker, we are less afraid to be drown'd, than thou art.

GONZALO: I'll warrant him for drowning, though the ship
were no stronger than a nutshell, and as leaky as an un-
stanched wench.

BOATSWAIN: Lay her a-hold, a-hold, set her two courses
off to sea again, lay her off.

Enter Mariners wet.

MARINERS: All lost, to prayers, to prayers, all lost.

BOATSWAIN: What must our mouths be cold?

GONZALO: The King and Prince, at prayers, let's assist
them,

For our case is as theirs.

SEBASTIAN: I'm out of patience.

ANTHONIO: We are merely cheated of our lives by drunk-
ards,

This wide-chop'd rascal, would thou mightst lie drowning

The washing of ten tides.

GONZALO: He'll be hang'd yet,

Though every drop of water swear against it,

And gape at wid'st to glut him.

A confused noise within.

Mercy on us.

We split, we split, farewell my wife, and children,

Farewell brother: we split, we split, we split.

ANTHONIO: Let's all sink wi' th' King.

SEBASTIAN: Let's take leave of him.

Exeunt.

GONZALO: Now would I give a thousand furlongs of sea,
for an acre of barren ground: long heath, brown furze,
any thing; the wills above be done, but I would fain die
a dry death.

Exit.

I.2

Enter Prospero and Miranda.

MIRANDA: If by your Art (my dearest father) you have

Put the wild waters in this roar, allay them:

The sky it seems would pour down stinking pitch,

But that the sea, mounting to th' welkin's cheek,

Dashes the fire out. Oh! I have suffered

With those that I saw suffer: a brave vessel

(Who had no doubt some noble creature in her)

Dash'd all to pieces: O the cry did knock
Against my very heart: poor souls, they perish'd.
Had I been any god of power, I would
Have sunk the sea within the earth, or ere
It should the good ship so have swallow'd, and
The fraughting souls within her.

PROSPERO: Be collected,
No more amazement: tell your piteous heart
There's no harm done.

MIRANDA: O woe, the day.

PROSPERO: No harm:
I have done nothing, but in care of thee
(Of thee my dear one; thee my daughter) who
Art ignorant of what thou art, nought knowing
Of whence I am: nor that I am more better
Than Prospero, master of a full poor cell.
And thy no greater father.

MIRANDA: More to know
Did never meddle with my thoughts.

PROSPERO: 'Tis time
I should inform thee farther: lend thy hand
And pluck my magic garment from me: so,
Lie there my Art: wipe thou thine eyes, have comfort,
The direful spectacle of the wrack which touch'd
The very virtue of compassion in thee:
I have with such provision in mine Art
So safely ordered, that there is no soul
No not so much perdition as an hair
Betid to any creature in the vessel
Which thou heard'st cry, which thou saw'st sink: sit
    down,
For thou must now know farther.

MIRANDA: You have often

Begun to tell me what I am, but stopp'd
And left me to a bootless inquisition,
Concluding, stay: not yet.

PROSPERO: The hour's now come.
The very minute bids thee ope thine ear,
Obey, and be attentive. Canst thou remember
A time before we came unto this cell?
I do not think thou canst, for then thou wast not
Out three years old.

MIRANDA: Certainly sir, I can.

PROSPERO: By what? by any other house, or person?
Of any thing the image, tell me, that
Hath kept with thy remembrance.

MIRANDA: 'Tis far off:
And rather like a dream, than an assurance
That my remembrance warrants: had I not
Four, or five women once, that tended me?

PROSPERO: Thou hadst; and more Miranda: but how is
it
That this lives in thy mind? What seest thou else
In the dark backward and abysm of Time?
If thou remember'st aught ere thou cam'st here,
How thou cam'st here thou mayst.

MIRANDA: But that I do not.

PROSPERO: Twelve year since, Miranda, twelve year since,
Thy father was the Duke of Milan and
A Prince of power.

MIRANDA: Sir, are not you my father?

PROSPERO: Thy mother was a piece of virtue, and
She said thou wast my daughter; and thy father
Was Duke of Milan, and his only heir,
A Princess; no worse issued.

MIRANDA: O the heavens.

What foul play had we, that we came from thence?
Or blessed was 't we did?
PROSPERO: Both, both my girl.
By foul play (as thou say'st) were we heav'd thence,
But blessedly holp hither.
MIRANDA: O my heart bleeds
To think o' th' teen that I have turn'd you to,
Which is from my remembrance; please you, farther.
PROSPERO: My brother and thy uncle, call'd Anthonio:
I pray thee mark me, that a brother should
Be so perfidious: he, whom next thyself
Of all the world I lov'd, and to him put
The manage of my state, as at that time
Through all the signories it was the first,
And Prospero, the prime Duke, being so reputed
In dignity; and for the liberal Arts,
Without a parallel; those being all my study,
The government I cast upon my brother,
And to my state grew stranger, being transported
And rapt in secret studies, thy false uncle
(Dost thou attend me?)
MIRANDA: Sir, most heedfully.
PROSPERO: Being once perfected how to grant suits,
How to deny them: who t' advance, and who
To trash for over-topping; new created
The creatures that were mine, I say, or chang'd 'em,
Or else new form'd 'em; having both the key,
Of officer, and office, set all hearts i' th' state
To what tune pleas'd his ear, that now he was
The ivy which had hid my princely trunk,
And suck'd my verdure out on 't: thou attend'st not?
MIRANDA: O good sir, I do.
PROSPERO: I pray thee mark me:

I thus neglecting worldly ends, all dedicated
To closeness, and the bettering of my mind
With that, which but by being so retir'd
O'er-priz'd all popular rate: in my false brother
Awak'd an evil nature, and my trust
Like a good parent, did beget of him
A falsehood in its contrary, as great
As my trust was, which had indeed no limit,
A confidence sans bound. He being thus lorded,
Not only with what my revenue yielded,
But what my power might else exact, like one
Who having into truth, by telling of it,
Made such a sinner of his memory
To credit his own lie, he did believe
He was indeed the Duke, out o' th' substitution
And executing th' outward face of royalty
With all prerogative: hence his ambition growing:
Dost thou hear?

MIRANDA: Your tale, sir, would cure deafness.

PROSPERO: To have no screen between this part he play'd,
And him he play'd it for, he needs will be
Absolute Milan. Me (poor man) my Library
Was Dukedom large enough: of temporal royalties
He thinks me now incapable. Confederates
(So dry he was for sway) wi' th' King of Naples
To give him annual tribute, do him homage,
Subject his coronet, to his crown and bend
The Dukedom yet unbow'd (alas poor Milan)
To most ignoble stooping.

MIRANDA: Oh the heavens!

PROSPERO: Mark his condition, and th' event, then tell me
If this might be a brother

MIRANDA: I should sin

To think but nobly of my grandmother,
Good wombs have borne bad sons.

PROSPERO: Now the condition.
This King of Naples being an enemy
To me inveterate, hearkens my brother's suit,
Which was, that he in lieu o' th' premises,
Of homage, and I know not how much tribute,
Should presently extirpate me and mine
Out of the Dukedom, and confer fair Milan
With all the honours, on my brother: whereon
A treacherous army levied, one midnight
Fated to th' purpose, did Anthonio open
The gates of Milan, and i' th' dead of darkness
The ministers for th' purpose hurried thence
Me, and thy crying self.

MIRANDA: Alack, for pity:
I not rememb'ring how I cried out then
Will cry it o'er again: it is a hint
That wrings mine eyes to 't.

PROSPERO: Hear a little further.
And then I'll bring thee to the present business
Which now's upon's: without the which, this story
Were most impertinent.

MIRANDA: Wherefore did they not
That hour destroy us?

PROSPERO: Well demanded, wench:
My tale provokes that question: dear, they durst not,
So dear the love my people bore me: nor set
A mark so bloody on the business; but
With colours fairer, painted their foul ends.
In few, they hurried us aboard a bark,
Bore us some leagues to sea, where they prepared
A rotten carcass of a butt, not rigg'd,

Nor tackle, sail, nor mast, the very rats
Instinctively have quit it: there they hoist us
To cry to th' sea, that roar'd to us; to sigh
To th' winds, whose pity sighing back again
Did us but loving wrong.

MIRANDA: Alack, what trouble
Was I then to you?

PROSPERO: O, a cherubin
Thou wast that did preserve me; thou didst smile,
Infused with a fortitude from heaven,
When I have deck'd the sea with drops full salt,
Under my burthen groan'd, which rais'd in me
An undergoing stomach, to bear up
Against what should ensue.

MIRANDA: How came we ashore?

PROSPERO: By Providence divine,
Some food, we had, and some fresh water, that
A noble Neapolitan Gonzalo
Out of his charity (who being then appointed
Master of this design) did give us, with
Rich garments, linens, stuffs, and necessaries
Which since have steaded much, so of his gentleness
Knowing I lov'd my books, he furnish'd me
From mine own Library, with volumes, that
I prize above my Dukedom.

MIRANDA: Would I might
But ever see that man.

PROSPERO: Now I arise,
Sit still, and hear the last of our sea-sorrow:
Here in this Island we arriv'd, and here
Have I, thy schoolmaster, made thee more profit
Than other Princess' can, that have more time
For vainer hours; and tutors, not so careful.

MIRANDA: Heaven thank you for 't. And now I pray you
　　sir,
　For still 'tis beating in my mind; your reason
　For raising this sea-storm?
PROSPERO: Know thus far forth,
　By accident most strange, bountiful Fortune
　(Now my dear Lady) hath mine enemies
　Brought to this shore: and by my prescience
　I find my zenith doth depend upon
　A most auspicious star, whose influence
　If now I court not, but omit, my fortunes
　Will ever after droop: here cease more questions,
　Thou art inclin'd to sleep: 'tis a good dulness,
　And give it away: I know thou canst not choose:
　Come away, servant, come; I am ready now,
　Approach my Ariel. Come.

Enter Ariel.

ARIEL: All hail, great Master, grave sir, hail: I come
　To answer thy best pleasure; be 't to fly,
　To swim, to dive into the fire: to ride
　On the curl'd clouds: to thy strong bidding, task
　Ariel, and all his quality.
PROSPERO: Hast thou, spirit.
　Perform'd to point, the tempest that I bade thee?
ARIEL: To every article.
　I boarded the King's ship: now on the beak,
　Now in the waist, the deck, in every cabin,
　I flam'd amazement, sometime I 'ld divide
　And burn in many places; on the topmast,
　The yards and boresprit, would I flame distinctly,
　Then meet, and join. Jove's lightning, the precursors
　O' th' dreadful thunder-claps more momentary
　And sight-outrunning were not; the fire, and cracks

Of sulphurous roaring, the most mighty Neptune
Seem to besiege, and make his bold waves tremble,
Yea, his dread trident shake.
PROSPERO: My brave spirit,
Who was so firm, so constant, that this coil
Would not infect his reason?
ARIEL: Not a soul
But felt a fever of the mad, and play'd
Some tricks of desperation; all but mariners
Plung'd in the foaming brine, and quit the vessel;
Then all afire with me the King's son Ferdinand
With hair up-staring (then like reeds, not hair)
Was the first man that leap'd; cried Hell is empty,
And all the devils are here.
PROSPERO: Why that's my spirit:
But was not this nigh shore?
ARIEL: Close by, my Master.
PROSPERO: But are they, Ariel, safe?
ARIEL: Not a hair perish'd:
On their sustaining garments not a blemish,
But fresher than before: and as thou bad'st me,
In troops I have dispers'd them 'bout the Isle:
The King's son have I landed by himself,
Whom I left cooling of the air with sighs,
In an odd angle of the Isle, and sitting
His arms in this sad knot.
PROSPERO: Of the King's ship,
The mariners, say how thou hast dispos'd,
And all the rest o' th' fleet?
ARIEL: Safely in harbour
Is the King's ship, in the deep nook, where once
Thou call'dst me up at midnight to fetch dew
From the still-vex'd Bermoothes, there she's hid;

The mariners all under hatches stowed,
Who, with a charm join'd to their suffer'd labour
I have left asleep: and for the rest o' th' fleet
(Which I dispers'd) they all have met again,
And are upon the Mediterranean flote
Bound sadly home for Naples,
Supposing that they saw the King's ship wrack'd,
And his great person perish.

PROSPERO: Ariel, thy charge
Exactly is perform'd; but there's more work:
What is the time o' th' day?

ARIEL: Past the mid season.

PROSPERO: At least two glasses: the time 'twixt six and
now
Must by us both be spent most preciously.

ARIEL: Is there more toil? Since thou dost give me pains,
Let me remember thee what thou hast promis'd,
Which is not yet perform'd me.

PROSPERO: How now? moody?
What is 't thou canst demand?

ARIEL: My liberty.

PROSPERO: Before the time be out? no more.

ARIEL: I prithee,
Remember I have done thee worthy service,
Told thee no lies, made thee no mistakings, serv'd
Without or grudge, or grumblings; thou didst promise
To bate me a full year.

PROSPERO: Dost thou forget
From what a torment I did free thee?

ARIEL: No.

PROSPERO: Thou dost: and think'st it much to tread the
ooze
Of the salt deep;

To run upon the sharp wind of the North,
To do me business in the veins o' th' earth
When it is bak'd with frost.

ARIEL: I do not sir.

PROSPERO: Thou liest, malignant Thing: hast thou forgot
The foul Witch Sycorax, who with age and envy
Was grown into a hoop? hast thou forgot her?

ARIEL: No sir.

PROSPERO: Thou hast: where was she born? speak: tell
me.

ARIEL: Sir, in Argier.

PROSPERO: O, was she so: I must
Once in a month recount what thou hast been,
Which thou forget'st. This damn'd Witch Sycorax
For mischiefs manifold, and sorceries terrible
To enter human hearing, from Argier
Thou know'st was banish'd: for one thing she did
They would not take her life: is not this true?

ARIEL: Ay, sir.

PROSPERO: This blue-ey'd hag, was hither brought with
child,
And here was left by th' sailors; thou my slave,
As thou report'st thyself, was then her servant,
And for thou wast a spirit too delicate
To act her earthy, and abhorr'd commands,
Refusing her grand hests, she did confine thee
By help of her more potent ministers,
And in her most unmitigable rage
Into a cloven pine, within which rift
Imprison'd, thou didst painfully remain
A dozen years: within which space she died,
And left thee there: where thou didst vent thy groans
As fast as mill-wheels strike: then was this Island

(Save for the son, that she did litter here,
A freckl'd whelp, hag-born) not honour'd with
A human shape.

ARIEL: Yes: Caliban her son.

PROSPERO: Dull thing, I say so: he, that Caliban
Whom now I keep in service: thou best know'st
What torment I did find thee in; thy groans
Did make wolves howl, and penetrate the breasts
Of ever-angry bears; it was a torment
To lay upon the damn'd, which Sycorax
Could not again undo: it was mine Art,
When I arriv'd, and heard thee, that made gape
The pine, and let thee out.

ARIEL: I thank thee Master.

PROSPERO: If thou more murmur'st, I will rend an oak
And peg thee in his knotty entrails, till
Thou hast howl'd away twelve winters.

ARIEL: Pardon, Master,
I will be correspondent to command
And do my spriting, gently.

PROSPERO: Do so: and after two days
I will discharge thee.

ARIEL: That's my noble Master:
What shall I do? say what? what shall I do?

PROSPERO: Go make thyself like a nymph o' th' sea, be
subject
To no sight but thine, and mine: invisible
To every eyeball else: go take this shape
And hither come in 't: go: hence with diligence.

Exit Ariel.

Awake, dear heart awake, thou hast slept well, Awake.

MIRANDA: The strangeness of your story, put
Heaviness in me.

PROSPERO: Shake it off: come on,
We'll visit Caliban, my slave, who never
Yields us kind answer.

MIRANDA: 'Tis a villain sir,
I do not love to look on.

PROSPERO: But as 'tis
We cannot miss him: he does make our fire,
Fetch in our wood, and serves in offices
That profit us: what hoa: slave: Caliban:
Thou earth, thou: speak.

CALIBAN *within*: There's wood enough within.

PROSPERO: Come forth I say, there's other business for
thee:
Come thou tortoise, when?
Enter Ariel like a water-nymph.
Fine apparition: my quaint Ariel,
Hark in thine ear.

ARIEL: My Lord, it shall be done.
Exit.

PROSPERO: Thou poisonous slave, got by the devil himself
Upon thy wicked dam; come forth.
Enter Caliban.

CALIBAN: As wicked dew, as e'er my mother brush'd
With raven's feather from unwholesome fen
Drop on you both: a South-west blow on ye,
And blister you all o'er.

PROSPERO: For this be sure, to-night thou shalt have
cramps,
Side-stitches, that shall pen thy breath up, urchins
Shall for that vast of night, that they may work
All exercise on thee: thou shalt be pinch'd
As thick as honeycomb, each pinch more stinging
Than bees that made 'em.

CALIBAN: I must eat my dinner:
  This Island's mine by Sycorax my mother,
  Which thou tak'st from me: when thou cam'st first
  Thou strok'dst me, and made much of me: wouldst give
    me
  Water with berries in 't: and teach me how
  To name the bigger Light, and how the less
  That burn by day, and night: and then I lov'd thee
  And show'd thee all the qualities o' th' Isle,
  The fresh springs, brine-pits, barren place and fertile;
  Curs'd be I that did so: all the charms
  Of Sycorax: toads, beetles, bats light on you:
  For I am all the subjects that you have,
  Which first was mine own King: and here you sty me
  In this hard rock, whiles you do keep from me
  The rest o' th' Island.
PROSPERO: Thou most lying slave,
  Whom stripes may move, not kindness: I have us'd
    thee
  (Filth as thou art) with humane care, and lodg'd thee
  In mine own cell, till thou didst seek to violate
  The honour of my child.
CALIBAN: Oh ho, oh ho, would 't had been done:
  Thou didst prevent me, I had peopled else
  This Isle with Calibans.
MIRANDA: Abhorred slave,
  Which any print of goodness wilt not take,
  Being capable of all ill: I pitied thee,
  Took pains to make thee speak, taught thee each hour
  One thing or other: when thou didst not (savage)
  Know thine own meaning; but wouldst gabble, like
  A thing most brutish, I endow'd thy purposes
  With words that made them known: but thy vile race

(Though thou didst learn) had that in 't, which good
  natures
Could not abide to be with; therefore wast thou
Deservedly confin'd into this rock,
Who hadst deserv'd more than a prison.

CALIBAN: You taught me language, and my profit on
  't
Is, I know how to curse: the red plague rid you
For learning me your language.

PROSPERO: Hag-seed, hence:
Fetch us in fuel, and be quick thou 'rt best
To answer other business: shrug'st thou, malice?
If thou neglect'st, or dost unwillingly
What I command, I'll rack thee with old cramps,
Fill all thy bones with aches, make thee roar,
That beasts shall tremble at thy din.

CALIBAN: No, pray thee.
I must obey, his Art is of such power,
It would control my dam's god Setebos,
And make a vassal of him.

PROSPERO: So slave, hence.

Exit Caliban.

Enter Ferdinand and Ariel, invisible, playing and singing.

ARIEL: *Song: Come unto these yellow sands,*
            And then take hands:
            Courtsied when you have, and kiss'd
              The wild waves whist:
            Foot it featly here, and there, and sweet Sprites bear
            The burthen

                              Burthen dispersedly
  Hark, hark, bow-wow: the watch-dogs bark, Bow-wow.
ARIEL: *Hark, hark, I hear, the strain of strutting Chanticleer*
            Cry cockadiddle-dow.

FERDINAND: Where should this music be? I' th' air, or
   th' earth?
  It sounds no more: and sure it waits upon
  Some god o' th' Island. Sitting on a bank,
  Weeping again the King my father's wrack,
  This music crept by me upon the waters,
  Allaying both their fury, and my passion
  With its sweet air: thence I have follow'd it
  (Or it hath drawn me rather) but 'tis gone.
  No, it begins again.

ARIEL *Song: Full fathom five thy father lies,*
        Of his bones are coral made:
        Those are pearls that were his eyes,
        Nothing of him that doth fade,
        But doth suffer a sea-change
        Into something rich, and strange:
        Sea-nymphs hourly ring his knell.
           Burthen: *Ding-dong.*
  Hark now I hear them, ding-dong bell.

FERDINAND: The ditty does remember my drown'd
   father;
  This is no mortal business, nor no sound
  That the earth owes: I hear it now above me.

PROSPERO: The fringed curtains of thine eye advance,
  And say what thou seest yond.

MIRANDA: What is 't a spirit?
  Lord, how it looks about: believe me sir,
  It carries a brave form. But 'tis a spirit.

PROSPERO: No wench, it eats, and sleeps, and hath such
   senses
  As we have: such. This gallant which thou seest
  Was in the wrack: and but he's something stain'd

With grief (that's beauty's canker) thou might'st call
   him
A goodly person: he hath lost his fellows,
And strays about to find 'em.
MIRANDA: I might call him
A thing divine, for nothing natural
I ever saw so noble.
PROSPERO: It goes on I see
As my soul prompts it: spirit, fine spirit, I'll free thee
Within two days for this.
FERDINAND: Most sure the goddess
On whom these airs attend: vouchsafe my prayer
May know if you remain upon this Island,
And that you will some good instruction give
How I may bear me here: my prime request
(Which I do last pronounce) is (O you wonder)
If you be maid, or no?
MIRANDA: No wonder, sir,
But certainly a maid.
FERDINAND: My language? heavens:
I am the best of them that speak this speech,
Were I but where 'tis spoken.
PROSPERO: How? the best?
What wert thou if the King of Naples heard thee?
FERDINAND: A single thing, as I am now, that wonders
To hear thee speak of Naples: he does hear me,
And that he does, I weep: myself am Naples,
Who, with mine eyes (never since at ebb) beheld
The King my father wrack'd.
MIRANDA: Alack, for mercy.
FERDINAND: Yes faith, and all his Lords, the Duke of
   Milan

And his brave son, being twain.

PROSPERO: The Duke of Milan
And his more braver daughter, could control thee
If now 'twere fit to do 't: at the first sight
They have chang'd eyes: delicate Ariel,
I'll set thee free for this. A word good sir,
I fear you have done yourself some wrong: a word.

MIRANDA: Why speaks my father so ungently? This
Is the third man that e'er I saw: the first
That e'er I sigh'd for: pity move my father
To be inclin'd my way.

FERDINAND: O, if a virgin,
And your affection not gone forth, I'll make you
The Queen of Naples.

PROSPERO: Soft sir, one word more.
They are both in either's powers: but this swift business
I must uneasy make, lest too light winning
Make the prize light. One word more: I charge thee
That thou attend me: thou dost here usurp
The name thou ow'st not, and hast put thyself
Upon this Island, as a spy, to win it
From me, the Lord on 't.

FERDINAND: No, as I am a man.

MIRANDA: There's nothing ill, can dwell in such a temple,
If the ill spirit have so fair a house,
Good things will strive to dwell with 't.

PROSPERO: Follow me.
Speak not you for him: he's a traitor: come,
I'll manacle thy neck and feet together:
Sea-water shalt thou drink: thy food shall be
The fresh-brook mussels, wither'd roots, and husks
Wherein the acorn cradled. Follow.

FERDINAND: No,

I will resist such entertainment, till
Mine enemy has more power.
      He draws, and is charmed from moving.
MIRANDA: O dear father,
  Make not too rash a trial of him, for
  He's gentle, and not fearful.
PROSPERO: What I say,
  My foot my tutor? Put thy sword up traitor,
  Who mak'st a show, but dar'st not strike: thy conscience
  Is so possess'd with guilt: come, from thy ward,
  For I can here disarm thee with this stick,
  And make thy weapon drop.
MIRANDA: Beseech you father.
PROSPERO: Hence: hang not on my garments.
MIRANDA: Sir have pity,
  I'll be his surety.
PROSPERO: Silence: one word more
  Shall make me chide thee, if not hate thee: what,
  An advocate for an impostor? hush:
  Thou think'st there is no more such shapes as he,
  (Having seen but him and Caliban:) foolish wench,
  To th' most of men, this is a Caliban,
  And they to him are angels.
MIRANDA: My affections
  Are then most humble: I have no ambition
  To see a goodlier man.
PROSPERO: Come on, obey:
  Thy nerves are in their infancy again,
  And have no vigour in them.
FERDINAND: So they are:
  My spirits, as in a dream, are all bound up:
  My father's loss, the weakness which I feel,
  The wrack of all my friends, nor this man's threats,

To whom I am subdu'd, are but light to me,
Might I but through my prison once a day
Behold this maid: all corners else o' th' Earth
Let liberty make use of: space enough
Have I in such a prison.

PROSPERO: It works: come on.
Thou hast done well, fine Ariel:
Follow me,
Hark what thou else shalt do me.

MIRANDA: Be of comfort,
My father's of a better nature, sir,
Than he appears by speech: this is unwonted
Which now came from him.

PROSPERO: Thou shalt be as free
As mountain winds; but then exactly do
All points of my command.

ARIEL: To th' syllable.

PROSPERO: Come follow: speak not for him.

Exeunt.

II. 1

Enter Alonso, Sebastian, Anthonio, Gonzalo, Adrian,
Francisco, and others.

GONZALO: Beseech you sir, be merry; you have cause
(So have we all) of joy; for our escape
Is much beyond our loss; our hint of woe
Is common, every day, some sailor's wife,
The masters of some merchant, and the merchant
Have just our theme of woe: but for the miracle,
(I mean our preservation) few in millions
Can speak like us: then wisely, good sir, weigh
Our sorrow, with our comfort.

ALONSO: Prithee peace.

SEBASTIAN: He receives comfort like cold porridge.

ANTHONIO: The visitor will not give him o'er so.

SEBASTIAN: Look, he's winding up the watch of his wit, by and by it will strike.

GONZALO: Sir.

SEBASTIAN: One: tell.

GONZALO: When every grief is entertain'd, that's offer'd
Comes to th' entertainer –

SEBASTIAN: A dollar.

GONZALO: Dolour comes to him indeed, you have spoken truer than you purpos'd.

SEBASTIAN: You have taken it wiselier than I meant you should.

GONZALO: Therefore my Lord –

ANTHONIO: Fie, what a spendthrift is he of his tongue.

ALONSO: I prithee spare.

GONZALO: Well, I have done: but yet –

SEBASTIAN: He will be talking.

ANTHONIO: Which, of he, or Adrian, for a good wager, first begins to crow?

SEBASTIAN: The old cock.

ANTHONIO: The cockerel.

SEBASTIAN: Done: the wager?

ANTHONIO: A laughter.

SEBASTIAN: A match.

ADRIAN: Though this Island seem to be desert –

SEBASTIAN: He, ha, ha.

ANTHONIO: So, you're paid.

ADRIAN: Uninhabitable, and almost inaccessible –

SEBASTIAN: Yet –

ADRIAN: Yet –

ANTHONIO: He could not miss 't.

ADRIAN: It must needs be of subtle, tender, and delicate temperance.

ANTHONIO: Temperance was a delicate wench.

SEBASTIAN: Ay, and a subtle, as he most learnedly deliver'd.

ADRIAN: The air breathes upon us here most sweetly.

SEBASTIAN: As if it had lungs, and rotten ones.

ANTHONIO: Or, as 'twere perfum'd by a fen.

GONZALO: Here is everything advantageous to life.

ANTHONIO: True, save means to live.

SEBASTIAN: Of that there's none, or little.

GONZALO: How lush and lusty the grass looks! How green!

ANTHONIO: The ground indeed is tawny.

SEBASTIAN: With an eye of green in 't.

ANTHONIO: He misses not much.

SEBASTIAN: No: he doth but mistake the truth totally.

GONZALO: But the rariety of it is, which is indeed almost beyond credit –

SEBASTIAN: As many vouch'd rarieties are.

GONZALO: That our garments being (as they were) drench'd in the sea, hold notwithstanding their freshness and glosses, being rather new-dy'd than stain'd with salt water.

ANTHONIO: If but one of his pockets could speak, would it not say he lies?

SEBASTIAN: Ay, or very falsely pocket up his report.

GONZALO: Methinks our garments are now as fresh as when we put them on first in Afric, at the marriage of the King's fair daughter Claribel to the King of Tunis.

SEBASTIAN: 'Twas a sweet marriage, and we prosper well in our return.

ADRIAN: Tunis was never grac'd before with such a paragon to their Queen.

GONZALO: Not since widow Dido's time.

ANTHONIO: Widow? A pox o' that: how came that widow in? Widow Dido!

SEBASTIAN: What if he had said widower Æneas too? Good Lord, how you take it?

ADRIAN: Widow Dido said you? you make me study of that: she was of Carthage, not of Tunis.

GONZALO: This Tunis sir was Carthage.

ADRIAN: Carthage?

GONZALO: I assure you Carthage.

ANTHONIO: His word is more than the miraculous harp.

SEBASTIAN: He hath rais'd the wall, and houses too.

ANTHONIO: What impossible matter will he make easy next?

SEBASTIAN: I think he will carry this Island home in his pocket, and give it his son for an apple.

ANTHONIO: And sowing the kernels of it in the sea, bring forth more islands.

GONZALO: Ay.

ANTHONIO: Why in good time.

GONZALO: Sir, we were talking, that our garments seem now as fresh as when we were at Tunis at the marriage of your daughter, who is now Queen.

ANTHONIO: And the rarest that e'er came there.

SEBASTIAN: Bate (I beseech you) widow Dido.

ANTHONIO: O widow Dido! Ay, widow Dido.

GONZALO: Is not sir my doublet as fresh as the first day I wore it? I mean in a sort.

ANTHONIO: That sort was well fish'd for.

GONZALO: When I wore it at your daughter's marriage.

ALONSO: You cram those words into mine ears, against
The stomach of my sense: would I had never
Married my daughter there: for coming thence

My son is lost, and (in my rate) she too,
Who is so far from Italy removed,
I ne'er again shall see her: O thou mine heir
Of Naples and of Milan, what strange fish
Hath made his meal on thee?

FRANCISCO: Sir he may live,
I saw him beat the surges under him,
And ride upon their backs; he trod the water
Whose enmity he flung aside: and breasted
The surge most swoln that met him: his bold head
'Bove the contentious waves he kept, and oared
Himself with his good arms in lusty stroke
To th' shore: that o'er his wave-worn basis bowed
As stooping to relieve him: I not doubt
He came alive to land.

ALONSO: No, no, he's gone.

SEBASTIAN: Sir you may thank yourself for this great loss,
That would not bless our Europe with your daughter,
But rather loose her to an African,
Where she at least, is banish'd from your eye,
Who hath cause to wet the grief on 't.

ALONSO: Prithee peace.

SEBASTIAN: You were kneel'd to, and importun'd other-
wise
By all of us: and the fair soul herself
Weigh'd between loathness, and obedience, at
Which end o' th' beam should bow: we have lost your
son,
I fear for ever: Milan and Naples have
Mo widows in them of this business making,
Than we bring men to comfort them:
The fault's your own.

ALONSO: So is the dear'st o' th' loss.

GONZALO: My Lord Sebastian,
   The truth you speak doth lack some gentleness,
   And time to speak it in: you rub the sore,
   When you should bring the plaster.
SEBASTIAN: Very well.
ANTHONIO: And most chirurgeonly.
GONZALO: It is foul weather in us all, good sir,
   When you are cloudy.
SEBASTIAN: Foul weather?
ANTHONIO: Very foul.
GONZALO: Had I plantation of this Isle my Lord –
ANTHONIO: He 'ld sow 't with nettle-seed
SEBASTIAN: Or docks, or mallows.
GONZALO: And were the King on 't, what would I do?
SEBASTIAN: 'Scape being drunk, for want of wine.
GONZALO: I' th' Commonwealth I would (by contraries)
   Execute all things: for no kind of traffic
   Would I admit: no name of magistrate:
   Letters should not be known: riches, poverty,
   And use of service, none: contract, succession,
   Bourn, bound of land, tilth, vineyard none:
   No use of metal, corn, or wine, or oil:
   No occupation, all men idle, all:
   And women too, but innocent and pure:
   No sovereignty.
SEBASTIAN: Yet he would be King on 't.
ANTHONIO: The latter end of his Commonwealth forgets
   the beginning.
GONZALO: All things in common Nature should produce
   Without sweat or endeavour: treason, felony,
   Sword, pike, knife, gun, or need of any engine
   Would I not have: but Nature should bring forth
   Of it own kind, all foison, all abundance

To feed my innocent people.

SEBASTIAN: No marrying 'mong his subjects?

ANTHONIO: None, man, all idle; whores and knaves.

GONZALO: I would with such perfection govern sir,
T' excel the Golden Age.

SEBASTIAN: 'Save his Majesty.

ANTHONIO: Long live Gonzalo:

GONZALO: And do you mark me, sir?

ALONSO: Prithee no more: thou dost talk nothing to me.

GONZALO: I do well believe your Highness, and did it to
minister occasion to these gentlemen, who are of such
sensible and nimble lungs, that they always use to laugh
at nothing.

ANTHONIO: 'Twas you we laugh'd at.

GONZALO: Who, in this kind of merry fooling am nothing
to you: so you may continue, and laugh at nothing still.

ANTHONIO: What a blow was there given!

SEBASTIAN: And it had not fallen flat-long.

GONZALO: You are gentlemen of brave mettle: you
would lift the Moon out of her sphere, if she would continue in it five weeks without changing.

Enter Ariel playing solemn music.

SEBASTIAN: We would so, and then go a bat-towling.

ANTHONIO: Nay good my Lord, be not angry.

GONZALO: No I warrant you, I will not adventure my
discretion so weakly: will you laugh me asleep, for I
am very heavy.

ANTHONIO: Go sleep, and hear us.

ALONSO: What, all so soon asleep? I wish mine eyes
Would, with themselves, shut up my thoughts, I find
They are inclin'd to do so.

SEBASTIAN: Please you sir,
Do not omit the heavy offer of it:

It seldom visits sorrow, when it doth,
It is a comforter.

ANTHONIO: We two my Lord,
Will guard your person, while you take your rest,
And watch your safety.

ALONSO: Thank you: wondrous heavy.

Exit Ariel.

SEBASTIAN: What a strange drowsiness possesses them!

ANTHONIO: It is the quality o' th' climate.

SEBASTIAN: Why
Doth it not then our eyelids sink? I find not
Myself dispos'd to sleep.

ANTHONIO: Nor I, my spirits are nimble
They fell together all, as by consent
They dropp'd, as by a thunder-stroke: what might
Worthy Sebastian?   O, what might?   No more:
And yet, methinks I see it in thy face,
What thou shouldst be: th' occasion speaks thee, and
My strong imagination sees a crown
Dropping upon thy head.

SEBASTIAN: What? Art thou waking?

ANTHONIO: Do you not hear me speak?

SEBASTIAN: I do, and surely
It is a sleepy language; and thou speak'st
Out of thy sleep: what is it thou didst say?
This is a strange repose, to be asleep
With eyes wide open: standing, speaking, moving:
And yet so fast asleep.

ANTHONIO: Noble Sebastian,
Thou let'st thy fortune sleep: die rather: wink'st
Whiles thou art waking.

SEBASTIAN: Thou dost snore distinctly.
There's meaning in thy snores.

ANTHONIO: I am more serious than my custom: you
    Must be so too, if heed me: which to do,
    Trebles thee o'er.

SEBASTIAN: Well: I am standing water.

ANTHONIO: I'll teach you how to flow.

SEBASTIAN: Do so: to ebb
    Hereditary sloth instructs me.

ANTHONIO: O!
    If you but knew how you the purpose cherish
    Whiles thus you mock it: how in stripping it
    You more invest it: ebbing men, indeed
    (Most often) do so near the bottom run
    By their own fear, or sloth.

SEBASTIAN: Prithee say on,
    The setting of thine eye, and cheek proclaim
    A matter from thee; and a birth, indeed,
    Which throes thee much to yield.

ANTHONIO: Thus sir:
    Although this Lord of weak remembrance; this
    Who shall be of as little memory
    When he is earth'd, hath here almost persuaded
    (For he's a spirit of persuasion, only
    Professes to persuade) the King his son's alive,
    'Tis as impossible that he's undrown'd,
    As he that sleeps here, swims.

SEBASTIAN: I have no hope
    That he's undrown'd.

ANTHONIO: O, out of that no hope,
    What great hope have you? No hope that way, is
    Another way so high a hope, that even
    Ambition cannot pierce a wink beyond
    But doubt discovery there. Will you grant with me
    That Ferdinand is drown'd?

SEBASTIAN: He's gone.

ANTHONIO: Then tell me,
Who's the next heir of Naples?

SEBASTIAN: Claribel.

ANTHONIO: She that is Queen of Tunis: she that
dwells
Ten leagues beyond man's life: she that from Naples
Can have no note, unless the Sun were post:
The Man i' th' Moon's too slow, till new-born chins
Be rough, and razorable; she that from whom
We all were sea-swallow'd, though some cast again
(And by that destiny) to perform an act
Whereof, what's past is prologue; what to come
In yours, and my discharge.

SEBASTIAN: What stuff is this? How say you?
'Tis true my brother's daughter's Queen of Tunis,
So is she heir of Naples, 'twixt which regions
There is some space.

ANTHONIO: A space, whose every cubit
Seems to cry out, how shall that Claribel
Measure us back to Naples? Keep in Tunis,
And let Sebastian wake. Say, this were death
That now hath seiz'd them, why they were no worse
Than now they are: there be that can rule Naples
As well as he that sleeps: Lords, that can prate
As amply, and unnecessarily
As this Gonzalo: I myself could make
A chough of as deep chat: O, that you bore
The mind that I do; what a sleep were this
For your advancement? Do you understand me?

SEBASTIAN: Methinks I do.

ANTHONIO: And how does your content
Tender your own good fortune?

SEBASTIAN: I remember
  You did supplant your brother Prospero.
ANTHONIO: True:
  And look how well my garments sit upon me,
  Much feater than before: my brother's servants
  Were then my fellows, now they are my men.
SEBASTIAN: But for your conscience.
ANTHONIO: Ay sir: where lies that? if 'twere a kibe
  'Twould put me to my slipper: but I feel not
  This deity in my bosom: twenty consciences
  That stand 'twixt me, and Milan, candied be they,
  And melt ere they molest: here lies your brother,
  No better than the earth he lies upon,
  If he were that which now he's like (that's dead)
  Whom I with this obedient steel (three inches of it)
  Can lay to bed for ever: whiles you doing thus,
  To the perpetual wink for aye might put
  This ancient morsel; this Sir Prudence, who
  Should not upbraid our course: for all the rest
  They'll take suggestion, as a cat laps milk,
  They'll tell the clock, to any business that
  We say befits the hour.
SEBASTIAN: Thy case, dear friend
  Shall be my precedent: as thou got'st Milan,
  I'll come by Naples: draw thy sword, one stroke
  Shall free thee from the tribute which thou payest,
  And I the King shall love thee.
ANTHONIO: Draw together:
  And when I rear my hand, do you the like
  To fall it on Gonzalo.
SEBASTIAN: O, but one word.
              Enter Ariel with music and song.
ARIEL: My master through his Art foresees the danger

That you (his friend) are in, and sends me forth
(For else his project dies) to keep them living.
        Sings in Gonzalo's ear.
        While you here do snoring lie,
        Open-ey'd Conspiracy
        His time doth take:
        If of life you keep a care,
        Shake off slumber and beware.
        Awake, awake.

ANTHONIO: Then let us both be sudden.

GONZALO: Now, good angels preserve the King.

ALONSO: Why how now, hoa; awake? Why are you
    drawn?
    Wherefore this ghastly looking?

GONZALO: What's the matter?

SEBASTIAN: Whiles we stood here securing your repose
    (Even now) we heard a hollow burst of bellowing
    Like bulls, or rather lions, did't not wake you?
    It struck mine ear most terribly.

ALONSO: I heard nothing.

ANTHONIO: O, 'twas a din to fright a monster's ear:
    To make an earthquake: sure it was the roar
    Of a whole herd of lions.

ALONSO: Heard you this Gonzalo?

GONZALO: Upon mine honour, sir, I heard a humming,
    (And that a strange one too) which did awake me:
    I shak'd you sir, and cried: as mine eyes open'd,
    I saw their weapons drawn: there was a noise,
    That's verily; 'tis best we stand upon our guard;
    Or that we quit this place: let's draw our weapons.

ALONSO: Lead off this ground and let's make further
    search
    For my poor son.

GONZALO: Heavens keep him from these beasts:
For he is sure i' th' Island.
ALONSO: Lead away.
ARIEL: Prospero my Lord, shall know what I have done.
So, King, go safely on to seek thy son.
Exeunt.

II. 2

Enter Caliban, with a burthen of wood. A noise of thunder heard.

CALIBAN: All the infections that the Sun sucks up
From bogs, fens, flats, on Prosper fall, and make him
By inch-meal a disease: his spirits hear me,
And yet I needs must curse. But they'll nor pinch,
Fright me with urchin-shows, pitch me i' th' mire,
Nor lead me like a firebrand, in the dark
Out of my way, unless he bid 'em; but
For every trifle, are they set upon me,
Sometime like apes, that mow and chatter at me,
And after bite me: then like hedgehogs, which
Lie tumbling in my barefoot way, and mount
Their pricks at my footfall: sometime am I
All wound with adders, who with cloven tongues
Do hiss me into madness. Lo, now, lo!
Enter Trinculo.
Here comes a spirit of his, and to torment me
For bringing wood in slowly: I 'll fall flat,
Perchance he will not mind me.
TRINCULO: Here's neither bush, nor shrub to bear off
any weather at all: and another storm brewing, I hear
it sing i' th' wind: yond same black cloud, yond huge
one, looks like a foul bombard, that would shed his

liquor: if it should thunder, as it did before, I know not where to hide my head: yond same cloud cannot choose but fall by pailfuls. What have we here, a man, or a fish? dead or alive? A fish, he smells like a fish: a very ancient and fish-like smell: a kind of, not of the newest Poor-John: a strange fish: were I in England now (as once I was) and had but this fish painted; not a holiday fool there but would give a piece of silver: there, would this monster, make a man: any strange beast there, makes a man: when they will not give a doit to relieve a lame beggar, they will lay out ten to see a dead Indian: legg'd like a man; and his fins like arms: warm o' my troth: I do now let loose my opinion; hold it no longer; this is no fish, but an islander, that hath lately suffered by a thunderbolt: alas, the storm is come again: my best way is to creep under his gaberdine: there is no other shelter hereabout: misery acquaints a man with strange bedfellows: I will here shroud till the dregs of the storm be past.

Enter Stephano singing.

STEPHANO: *I shall no more to sea, to sea, here shall I die a-shore.*

This is a very scurvy tune to sing at a man's funeral: well, here's my comfort.

Drinks.

Sings.

The master, the swabber, the boatswain and I;
The gunner, and his mate
Lov'd Mall, Meg, and Marian, and Margery,
But none of us car'd for Kate.
For she had a tongue with a tang,
Would cry to a sailor go hang:
She lov'd not the savour of tar nor of pitch,

Yet a tailor might scratch her where'er she did itch.
Then to sea boys, and let her go hang.
This is a scurvy tune too; but here's my comfort.
                              Drinks.

CALIBAN: Do not torment me: oh.

STEPHANO: What's the matter? Have we devils here? Do
you put tricks upon 's with salvages, and men of Ind?
ha? I have not 'scap'd drowning, to be afeard now of
your four legs: for it hath been said; as proper a man as
ever went on four legs, cannot make him give ground:
and it shall be said so again, while Stephano breathes at
nostrils.

CALIBAN: The spirit torments me: oh.

STEPHANO: This is some monster of the Isle, with four
legs; who hath got (as I take it) an ague: where the devil
should he learn our language? I will give him some
relief if it be but for that: if I can recover him, and keep
him tame, and get to Naples with him, he's a present
for any Emperor that ever trod on neat's-leather.

CALIBAN: Do not torment me prithee: I'll bring my
wood home faster.

STEPHANO: He's in his fit now; and does not talk after
the wisest; he shall taste of my bottle: if he have never
drunk wine afore, it will go near to remove his fit: if
I can recover him, and keep him tame, I will not take
too much for him; he shall pay for him that hath him,
and that soundly.

CALIBAN: Thou dost me yet but little hurt; thou wilt
anon, I know it by thy trembling: now Prosper works
upon thee.

STEPHANO: Come on your ways: open your mouth: here
is that which will give language to you cat; open your
mouth; this will shake your shaking, I can tell you, and

that soundly: you cannot tell who's your friend; open your chaps again.

TRINCULO: I should know that voice: it should be, but he is drown'd; and these are devils; O defend me.

STEPHANO: Four legs and two voices; a most delicate monster: his forward voice now is to speak well of his friend; his backward voice, is to utter foul speeches, and to detract: if all the wine in my bottle will recover him, I will help his ague: come: Amen, I will pour some in thy other mouth.

TRINCULO: Stephano.

STEPHANO: Doth thy other mouth call me? Mercy, mercy: this is a devil, and no monster: I will leave him, I have no long spoon.

TRINCULO: Stephano: if thou beest Stephano, touch me, and speak to me: for I am Trinculo; be not afeard, thy good friend Trinculo.

STEPHANO: If thou beest Trinculo: come forth: I'll pull thee by the lesser legs; if any be Trinculo's legs, these are they: thou art very Trinculo indeed: how cam'st thou to be the siege of this moon-calf? Can he vent Trinculos?

TRINCULO: I took him to be kill'd with a thunderstroke; but art thou not drown'd Stephano: I hope now thou art not drown'd: is the storm over-blown? I hid me under the dead mooncalf's gaberdine, for fear of the storm: and art thou living Stephano? O Stephano, two Neapolitans scap'd?

STEPHANO: Prithee do not turn me about, my stomach is not constant.

CALIBAN: These be fine things, and if they be not sprites: that's a brave god, and bears celestial liquor: I will kneel to him.

STEPHANO: How didst thou scape? How cam'st thou

hither? Swear by this bottle how thou cam'st hither: I escap'd upon a butt of sack, which the sailors heaved o'erboard, by this bottle which I made of the bark of a tree, with mine own hands, since I was cast ashore.

CALIBAN: I'll swear upon that bottle, to be thy true subject, for the liquor is not earthly.

STEPHANO: Here: swear then how thou escap'dst.

TRINCULO: Swum ashore, man, like a duck: I can swim like a duck I'll be sworn.

STEPHANO: Here, kiss the book. Though thou canst swim like a duck, thou art made like a goose.

TRINCULO: O Stephano, hast any more of this?

STEPHANO: The whole butt, man, my cellar is in a rock by th' sea-side, where my wine is hid: how now moon-calf, how does thine ague?

CALIBAN: Hast thou not dropp'd from heaven?

STEPHANO: Out o' th' Moon I do assure thee. I was the Man i' th' Moon, when time was.

CALIBAN: I have seen thee in her; and I do adore thee: my Mistress show'd me thee, and thy dog, and thy bush.

STEPHANO: Come, swear to that: kiss the book: I will furnish it anon with new contents: swear.

TRINCULO: By this good light, this is a very shallow monster: I afeard of him? A very weak monster: the Man i' th' Moon? A most poor credulous monster: well drawn monster, in good sooth.

CALIBAN: I'll show thee every fertile inch o' th' Island: and I will kiss thy foot: I prithee be my god.

TRINCULO: By this light, a most perfidious, and drunken monster, when 's god's asleep he'll rob his bottle.

CALIBAN: I'll kiss thy foot. I'll swear myself thy subject.

STEPHANO: Come on then: down and swear.

TRINCULO: I shall laugh myself to death at this puppy-headed monster: a most scurvy monster: I could find in my heart to beat him.

STEPHANO: Come, kiss.

TRINCULO: But that the poor monster's in drink: an abominable monster.

CALIBAN: I'll show thee the best springs: I'll pluck thee
 berries:
 I'll fish for thee; and get thee wood enough.
 A plague upon the tyrant that I serve;
 I'll bear him no more sticks, but follow thee,
 Thou wondrous man.

TRINCULO: A most ridiculous monster, to make a wonder of a poor drunkard.

CALIBAN: I prithee let me bring thee where crabs grow;
 And I with my long nails will dig thee pig-nuts;
 Show thee a jay's nest, and instruct thee how
 To snare the nimble marmoset: I'll bring thee
 To clustering filberts, and sometimes I'll get thee
 Young scamels from the rock : wilt thou go with
 me?

STEPHANO: I prithee now lead the way without any more talking. Trinculo, the King, and all our company else being drown'd, we will inherit here: here; bear my bottle: fellow Trinculo; we'll fill him by and by again.

CALIBAN: *sings drunkenly:* Farewell master; farewell, farewell.

TRINCULO: A howling monster: a drunken monster.

CALIBAN: *No more dams I'll make for fish,*
 Nor fetch in firing, at requiring,
 Nor scrape trenchering, nor wash dish,
 Ban' ban' Cacaliban
 Has a new master, get a new man.

Freedom, high-day, high-day freedom, freedom high-
day, freedom.

STEPHANO: O brave monster: lead the way.

Exeunt.

III. 1

Enter Ferdinand (bearing a log).

FERDINAND: There be some sports are painful; and their
labour
Delight in them sets off: some kinds of baseness
Are nobly undergone; and most poor matters
Point to rich ends: this my mean task
Would be as heavy to me, as odious, but
The Mistress which I serve, quickens what's dead,
And makes my labours, pleasures: O she is
Ten times more gentle, than her father's crabbed;
And he's compos'd of harshness. I must remove
Some thousands of these logs, and pile them up,
Upon a sore injunction; my sweet Mistress
Weeps when she sees me work, and says, such baseness
Had never like executor: I forget:
But these sweet thoughts, do even refresh my labours,
Most busy lest, when I do it.

Enter Miranda, and Prospero above.

MIRANDA: Alas, now pray you
Work not so hard: I would the lightning had
Burnt up those logs that you are enjoin'd to pile:
Pray set it down, and rest you: when this burns
'Twill weep for having wearied you: my father
Is hard at study; pray now rest yourself,
He's safe for these three hours.

FERDINAND: O most dear Mistress,

The Sun will set before I shall discharge
What I must strive to do.
MIRANDA: If you'll sit down
I'll bear your logs the while: pray give me that,
I'll carry it to the pile.
FERDINAND: No precious creature,
I had rather crack my sinews, break my back,
Than you should such dishonour undergo,
While I sit lazy by.
MIRANDA: It would become me
As well as it does you; and I should do it
With much more ease: for my good will is to it,
And yours it is against.
PROSPERO: Poor worm thou art infected,
This visitation shows it.
MIRANDA: You look wearily.
FERDINAND: No, noble Mistress, 'tis fresh morning with
me
When you are by at night: I do beseech you
Chiefly, that I might set it in my prayers,
What is your name?
MIRANDA: Miranda, O my father,
I have broke your hest to say so.
FERDINAND: Admir'd Miranda,
Indeed the top of admiration, worth
What's dearest to the world: full many a Lady
I have eye'd with best regard, and many a time
Th' harmony of their tongues, hath into bondage
Brought my too diligent ear: for several virtues
Have I lik'd several women, never any
With so full soul, but some defect in her
Did quarrel with the noblest grace she ow'd,
And put it to the foil. But you, O you,

So perfect, and so peerless, are created
Of every creature's best.

MIRANDA: I do not know
One of my sex; no woman's face remember,
Save from my glass, mine own: nor have I seen
More that I may call men, than you good friend,
And my dear father: how features are abroad
I am skilless of; but by my modesty
(The jewel in my dower) I would not wish
Any companion in the world but you:
Nor can imagination form a shape
Besides yourself, to like of: but I prattle
Something too wildly, and my father's precepts
I therein do forget.

FERDINAND: I am, in my condition
A Prince, Miranda, I do think a King
(I would not so) and would no more endure
This wooden slavery, than to suffer
The flesh-fly blow my mouth: hear my soul speak.
The very instant that I saw you, did
My heart fly to your service, there resides
To make me slave to it, and for your sake
Am I this patient log-man.

MIRANDA: Do you love me?

FERDINAND: O heaven; O earth, bear witness to this
sound,
And crown what I profess with kind event
If I speak true: if hollowly, invert
What best is boded me, to mischief: I,
Beyond all limit of what else i' th' world
Do love, prize, honour you.

MIRANDA: I am a fool
To weep at what I am glad of.

PROSPERO: Fair encounter
  Of two most rare affections: heavens rain grace
  On that which breeds between 'em.
FERDINAND: Wherefore weep you?
MIRANDA: At mine unworthiness, that dare not offer
  What I desire to give; and much less take
  What I shall die to want: but this is trifling,
  And all the more it seeks to hide itself,
  The bigger bulk it shows. Hence bashful cunning,
  And prompt me plain and holy innocence.
  I am your wife, if you will marry me;
  If not, I'll die your maid: to be your fellow
  You may deny me, but I'll be your servant
  Whether you will or no.
FERDINAND: My Mistress, dearest,
  And I thus humble ever.
MIRANDA: My husband, then?
FERDINAND: Ay, with a heart as willing
  As bondage e'er of freedom: here's my hand.
MIRANDA: And mine, with my heart in 't; and now fare-
    well
  Till half an hour hence.
FERDINAND: A thousand, thousand.
                    Exeunt.
PROSPERO: So glad of this as they I cannot be,
  Who are surpris'd with all; but my rejoicing
  At nothing can be more: I'll to my book,
  For yet ere supper-time, must I perform
  Much business appertaining.
                    Exit.

III. 2

Enter Caliban, Stephano, and Trinculo.

STEPHANO: Tell not me, when the butt is out we will drink water, not a drop before; therefore bear up, and board 'em. Servant-monster, drink to me.

TRINCULO: Servant-monster? The folly of this Island, they say there's but five upon this Isle; we are three of them, if th' other two be brain'd like us, the State totters.

STEPHANO: Drink servant-monster when I bid thee, thy eyes are almost set in thy head. .

TRINCULO: Where should they be set else? he were a brave monster indeed, if they were set in his tail.

STEPHANO: My man-monster hath drown'd his tongue in sack: for my part the sea cannot drown me, I swam ere I could recover the shore, five-and-thirty leagues off and on, by this light thou shalt be my lieutenant monster, or my standard.

TRINCULO: Your lieutenant if you list, he's no standard.

STEPHANO: We'll not run Monsieur Monster.

TRINCULO: Nor go neither: but you'll lie like dogs, and yet say nothing neither.

STEPHANO: Moon-calf, speak once in thy life, if thou beest a good moon-calf.

CALIBAN: How does thy honour? Let me lick thy shoe: I'll not serve him, he is not valiant.

TRINCULO: Thou liest most ignorant monster, I am in case to justle a constable: why, thou debosh'd fish thou, was there ever man a coward, that hath drunk so much sack as I to-day? Wilt thou tell a monstrous lie, being but half a fish, and half a monster?

CALIBAN: Lo, how he mocks me, wilt thou let him my Lord?

TRINCULO: Lord, quoth he? That a monster should be such a natural!

CALIBAN: Lo, lo again: bite him to death I prithee.

STEPHANO: Trinculo, keep a good tongue in your head: if you prove a mutineer, the next tree: the poor monster's my subject, and he shall not suffer indignity.

CALIBAN: I thank my noble Lord. Wilt thou be pleas'd to hearken once again to the suit I made to thee?

STEPHANO: Marry will I: kneel, and repeat it, I will stand, and so shall Trinculo.

Enter Ariel invisible.

CALIBAN: As I told thee before, I am subject to a tyrant, a sorcerer, that by his cunning hath cheated me of the Island.

ARIEL: Thou liest.

CALIBAN: Thou liest, thou jesting monkey thou
I would my valiant master would destroy thee.
I do not lie.

STEPHANO: Trinculo, if you trouble him any more in 's tale, by this hand, I will supplant some of your teeth.

TRINCULO: Why, I said nothing.

STEPHANO: Mum then, and no more: proceed.

CALIBAN: I say by sorcery he got this Isle
From me, he got it. If thy greatness will
Revenge it on him (for I know thou dar'st)
But this Thing dare not.

STEPHANO: That's most certain.

CALIBAN: Thou shalt be Lord of it, and I'll serve thee.

STEPHANO: How now shall this be compass'd? Canst thou bring me to the party?

CALIBAN: Yea, yea my Lord, I'll yield him thee asleep,
Where thou mayst knock a nail into his head.

ARIEL: Thou liest, thou canst not.

CALIBAN: What a pied ninny's this? Thou scurvy patch:
I do beseech thy greatness give him blows,
And take his bottle from him: when that's gone,
He shall drink nought but brine, for I'll not show him
Where the quick freshes are.

STEPHANO: Trinculo, run into no further danger: inter-
rupt the monster one word further, and by this hand, I'll
turn my mercy out o' doors, and make a stock-fish of
thee.

TRINCULO: Why, what did I? I did nothing: I'll go
farther off.

STEPHANO: Didst thou not say he lied?

ARIEL: Thou liest.

STEPHANO: Do I so? Take thou that,
As you like this, give me the lie another time.

TRINCULO: I did not give the lie: out o' your wits, and
hearing too? A pox o' your bottle, this can sack and
drinking do: a murrain on your monster, and the devil
take your fingers.

CALIBAN: Ha, ha, ha.

STEPHANO: Now forward with your tale: prithee stand
further off.

CALIBAN: Beat him enough: after a little time
I'll beat him too.

STEPHANO: Stand farther: come proceed.

CALIBAN: Why, as I told thee, 'tis a custom with him
I' th' afternoon to sleep: there thou mayst brain him,
Having first seiz'd his books: or with a log
Batter his skull, or paunch him with a stake,
Or cut his wezand with thy knife. Remember
First to possess his books; for without them
He's but a sot, as I am; nor hath not

One spirit to command: they all do hate him
As rootedly as I. Burn but his books,
He has brave utensils (for so he calls them)
Which when he has a house, he'll deck withal.
And that most deeply to consider, is
The beauty of his daughter: he himself
Calls her a nonpareil: I never saw a woman
But only Sycorax my dam, and she;
But she as far surpasseth Sycorax,
As great'st does least.

STEPHANO: Is it so brave a lass?

CALIBAN: Ay Lord, she will become thy bed, I warrant,
And bring thee forth brave brood.

STEPHANO: Monster, I will kill this man: his daughter
and I will be King and Queen, save our Graces: and
Trinculo and thyself shall be Viceroys: dost thou like
the plot, Trinculo?

TRINCULO. Excellent.

STEPHANO: Give me thy hand, I am sorry I beat thee: but
while thou liv'st keep a good tongue in thy head.

CALIBAN: Within this half hour will he be asleep,
Wilt thou destroy him then?

STEPHANO: Ay on mine honour.

ARIEL: This will I tell my Master.

CALIBAN: Thou mak'st me merry: I am full of pleasure,
Let us be jocund. Will you troll the catch
You taught me but while-ere?

STEPHANO: At thy request monster I will do reason, any
reason: come on Trinculo, let us sing.

Sings.

Flout 'em, and cout 'em: and scout 'em and flout 'em.
Thought is free.

CALIBAN: That's not the tune.

Ariel plays the tune on a tabor and pipe.

STEPHANO: What is this same?

TRINCULO: This is the tune of our catch, played by the picture of Nobody.

STEPHANO: If thou beest a man, show thyself in thy likeness: if thou beest a devil, take 't as thou list.

TRINCULO: O forgive me my sins.

STEPHANO: He that dies pays all debts: I defy thee; mercy upon us.

CALIBAN: Art thou afeard?

STEPHANO: No monster, not I.

CALIBAN: Be not afeard, the Isle is full of noises,
Sounds, and sweet airs, that give delight and hurt not:
Sometimes a thousand twangling instruments
Will hum about mine ears; and sometimes voices,
That if I then had wak'd after long sleep,
Will make me sleep again, and then in dreaming,
The clouds methought would open, and show riches
Ready to drop upon me, that when I wak'd
I cried to dream again.

STEPHANO: This will prove a brave kingdom to me,
Where I shall have my music for nothing.

CALIBAN: When Prospero is destroy'd.

STEPHANO: That shall be by and by: I remember the story.

TRINCULO: The sound is going away, let's follow it, and after do our work.

STEPHANO: Lead monster, we'll follow: I would I could see this taborer, he lays it on.

TRINCULO: Wilt come? I'll follow Stephano.

Exeunt.

III. 3

Enter Alonso, Sebastian, Anthonio, Gonzalo, Adrian,
Francisco, and others.

GONZALO: By 'r lakin, I can go no further, sir,
My old bones aches: here's a maze trod indeed
Through forth-rights, and meanders: by your patience,
I needs must rest me.

ALONSO: Old Lord, I cannot blame thee,
Who am myself attach'd with weariness
To th' dulling of my spirits: sit down, and rest:
Even here I will put off my hope, and keep it
No longer for my flatterer: he is drown'd
Whom thus we stray to find, and the sea mocks
Our frustrate search on land: well, let him go.

ANTHONIO: I am right glad, that he's so out of hope:
Do not for one repulse forego the purpose
That you resolv'd t' effect.

SEBASTIAN: The next advantage will we take throughly.

ANTHONIO: Let it be to-night,
For now they are oppress'd with travel, they
Will not, nor cannot use such vigilance
As when they are fresh.

SEBASTIAN: I say to-night: no more.

Solemn and strange music: and Prospero on the top (invisible).
Enter several strange shapes, bringing in a banquet; and dance
about it with gentle actions of salutations, and inviting the King,
etc., to eat, they depart.

ALONSO: What harmony is this? My good friends, hark.

GONZALO: Marvellous sweet music.

ALONSO: Give us kind keepers, heavens: what were these?

SEBASTIAN: A living drollery: now I will believe

That there are unicorns: that in Arabia
There is one tree, the Phœnix' throne, one Phœnix
At this hour reigning there.

ANTHONIO: I'll believe both:
And what does else want credit, come to me
And I'll be sworn 'tis true: travellers ne'er did lie,
Though fools at home condemn 'em.

GONZALO: If in Naples
I should report this now, would they believe me?
If I should say I saw such Islanders;
(For certes, these are people of the Island)
Who though they are of monstrous shape, yet note
Their manners are more gentle, kind, than of
Our human generation you shall find
Many, nay almost any.

PROSPERO: Honest Lord,
Thou hast said well: for some of you there present
Are worse than devils.

ALONSO: I cannot too much muse
Such shapes, such gesture, and such sound expressing
(Although they want the use of tongue) a kind
Of excellent dumb discourse.

PROSPERO: Praise in departing.

FRANCISCO: They vanish'd strangely.

SEBASTIAN: No matter, since
They have left their viands behind; for we have stomachs.
Will 't please you taste of what is here?

ALONSO: Not I.

GONZALO: Faith sir, you need not fear: when we were
boys
Who would believe that there were mountaineers,
Dew-lapp'd, like bulls, whose throats had hanging at 'em
Wallets of flesh? Or that there were such men

Whose heads stood in their breasts? which now we find
Each putter-out of five for one, will bring us
Good warrant of.
ALONSO: I will stand to, and feed,
Although my last, no matter, since I feel
The best is past: brother: my Lord, the Duke,
Stand to, and do as we.

Thunder and lightning. Enter Ariel (like a harpy) claps his wings upon the table, and with a quaint device the banquet vanishes.

ARIEL: You are three men of sin, whom Destiny
That hath to instrument this lower world,
And what is in 't, the never-surfeited sea,
Hath caus'd to belch up you; and on this Island,
Where man doth not inhabit, you 'mongst men,
Being most unfit to live: I have made you mad;
And even with such-like valour, men hang, and drown
Their proper selves: you fools, I and my fellows
Are ministers of Fate, the elements
Of whom your swords are temper'd, may as well
Wound the loud winds, or with bemock'd-at stabs
Kill the still-closing waters, as diminish
One dowle that's in my plume; my fellow-ministers
Are like invulnerable: if you could hurt,
Your swords are now too massy for your strengths,
And will not be uplifted: but remember
(For that's my business to you) that you three
From Milan did supplant good Prospero,
Expos'd unto the sea (which hath requit it)
Him, and his innocent child: for which foul deed,
The Powers, delaying (not forgetting) have
Incens'd the seas, and shores: yea, all the creatures
Against your peace: thee of thy son, Alonso
They have bereft; and do pronounce by me

Lingering perdition (worse than any death
Can be at once) shall step by step attend
You, and your ways, whose wraths to guard you from,
Which here, in this most desolate Isle, else falls
Upon your heads, is nothing but heart's sorrow,
And a clear life ensuing.

*He vanishes in thunder: then (to soft music) enter the shapes
again, and dance (with mocks and mows) and carrying out the
table.*

PROSPERO: Bravely the figure of this harpy, hast thou
Perform'd, my Ariel, a grace it had devouring:
Of my instruction, hast thou nothing bated
In what thou hadst to say: so with good life,
And observation strange, my meaner ministers
Their several kinds have done: my high charms work,
And these (mine enemies) are all knit up
In their distractions: they now are in my power;
And in these fits, I leave them, while I visit
Young Ferdinand (whom they suppose is drown'd)
And his, and mine lov'd darling.

Exit above.

GONZALO: I' th' name of something holy, sir, why stand
you
In this strange stare?

ALONSO: O, it is monstrous: monstrous:
Methought the billows spoke, and told me of it,
The winds did sing it to me: and the thunder
(That deep and dreadful organ-pipe) pronounc'd
The name of Prosper: it did bass my trespass,
Therefore my son i' th' ooze is bedded; and
I'll seek him deeper than e'er plummet sounded,
And with him there lie mudded.

Exit.

SEBASTIAN: But one fiend at a time,
   I'll fight their legions o'er.
ANTHONIO: I'll be thy second.
                    Exeunt.
GONZALO: All three of them are desperate: their great guilt
   (Like poison given to work a great time after)
   Now 'gins to bite the spirits: I do beseech you
   (That are of suppler joints) follow them swiftly
   And hinder them from what this ecstasy
   May now provoke them to.
ADRIAN: Follow, I pray you.
                    Exeunt omnes.

IV. I

Enter Prospero, Ferdinand, and Miranda.
PROSPERO: If I have too austerely punish'd you,
   Your compensation makes amends, for I
   Have given you here, a third of mine own life,
   Or that for which I live: who, once again
   I tender to thy hand: all thy vexations
   Were but my trials of thy love, and thou
   Hast strangely stood the test: here, afore heaven
   I ratify this my rich gift: O Ferdinand,
   Do not smile at me, that I boast her off,
   For thou shalt find she will outstrip all praise
   And make it halt, behind her.
FERDINAND: I do believe it
   Against an oracle.
PROSPERO: Then, as my gift, and thine own acquisition
   Worthily purchas'd, take my daughter: but
   If thou dost break her virgin-knot, before
   All sanctimonious ceremonies may

With full and holy rite, be minister'd,
No sweet aspersion shall the heavens let fall
To make this contract grow; but barren hate,
Sour-ey'd disdain, and discord shall bestrew
The union of your bed, with weeds so loathly
That you shall hate it both: therefore take heed,
As Hymen's lamps shall light you.

FERDINAND: As I hope
For quiet days, fair issue, and long life,
With such love, as 'tis now, the murkiest den,
The most opportune place, the strong'st suggestion,
Our worser genius can, shall never melt
Mine honour into lust, to take away
The edge of that day's celebration,
When I shall think, or Phœbus' steeds are founder'd,
Or Night kept chain'd below.

PROSPERO: Fairly spoke;
. Sit then, and talk with her, she is thine own;
What Ariel; my industrious servant Ariel.

Enter Ariel.

ARIEL: What would my potent master? Here I am.

PROSPERO: Thou, and thy meaner fellows, your last service
Did worthily perform: and I must use you
In such another trick: go bring the rabble
(O'er whom I give thee power) here, to this place:
Incite them to quick motion, for I must
Bestow upon the eyes of this young couple
Some vanity of mine Art: it is my promise,
And they expect it from me.

ARIEL: Presently?

PROSPERO: Ay: with a twink.

ARIEL: Before you can say come, and go,
And breathe twice; and cry, so so:

Each one tripping on his toe,
Will be here with mop, and mow,
Do you love me Master? No?

PROSPERO: Dearly, my delicate Ariel: do not approach
Till thou dost hear me call.

ARIEL: Well: I conceive.

Exit.

PROSPERO: Look thou be true: do not give dalliance
Too much the rein: the strongest oaths, are straw
To th' fire i' th' blood: be more abstemious,
Or else good night your vow.

FERDINAND: I warrant you, sir,
The white cold virgin snow, upon my heart
Abates the ardour of my liver.

PROSPERO: Well.
Now come my Ariel, bring a corollary,
Rather than want a spirit; appear, and pertly.

Soft music.

No tongue: all eyes: be silent.

Enter Iris.

IRIS: Ceres, most bounteous Lady, thy rich leas
Of wheat, rye, barley, vetches, oats and pease;
Thy turfy mountains, where live nibbling sheep,
And flat meads thatch'd with stover, them to keep:
Thy banks with pioned, and twilled brims
Which spongy April, at thy hest betrims,
To make cold nymphs chaste crowns; and thy broom-
    groves;
Whose shadow the dismissed bachelor loves,
Being lass-lorn: thy pole-clipt vineyard,
And thy sea-marge sterile, and rocky-hard,
Where thou thyself dost air, the Queen o' the sky,
Whose watery arch, and messenger, am I,

Bids thee leave these, and with her sovereign grace,
Here on this grass-plot, in this very place
To come, and sport: here peacocks fly amain:
Approach, rich Ceres, here to entertain.

Enter Ceres.

CERES: Hail, many-coloured messenger, that ne'er
Dost disobey the wife of Jupiter:
Who, with thy saffron wings, upon my flowers
Diffusest honey-drops, refreshing showers,
And with each end of thy blue bow dost crown
My bosky acres, and my unshrubb'd down,
Rich scarf to my proud earth: why hath thy Queen
Summon'd me hither, to this short-grass'd green?

IRIS: A contract of true love, to celebrate,
And some donation freely to estate
On the blest lovers.

CERES: Tell me heavenly Bow,
If Venus or her son, as thou dost know,
Do now attend the Queen? Since they did plot
The means, that dusky Dis, my daughter got,
Her, and her blind boy's scandal'd company,
I have forsworn.

IRIS: Of her society
Be not afraid: I met her deity
Cutting the clouds towards Paphos: and her son
Dove-drawn with her: here thought they to have done
Some wanton charm, upon this man and maid,
Whose vows are, that no bed-right shall be paid
Till Hymen's torch be lighted: but in vain,
Mars's hot minion is return'd again,
Her waspish-headed son, has broke his arrows,
Swears he will shoot no more, but play with sparrows,
And be a boy right out.

CERES: Highest Queen of State,
    Great Juno comes, I know her by her gait.
                Enter Juno.

JUNO: How does my bounteous sister? Go with me
    To bless this twain, that they may prosperous be,
    And honour'd in their issue.
                They sing.

JUNO: *Honour, riches, marriage, blessing,*
    Long continuance, and increasing,
    Hourly joys, be still upon you,
    Juno sings her blessings on you.

CERES: *Earth's increase, foison plenty,*
    Barns, and garners, never empty,
    Vines, with clustering bunches growing,
    Plants, with goodly burthen bowing:
    Spring come to you at the farthest,
    In the very end of harvest.
    Scarcity and want shall shun you,
    Ceres' blessing so is on you.

FERDINAND: This is a most majestic vision, and
    Harmonious charmingly: may I be bold
    To think these spirits?

PROSPERO: Spirits, which by mine Art
    I have from their confines call'd to enact
    My present fancies.

FERDINAND: Let me live here ever,
    So rare a wonder'd father, and a wise
    Makes this place Paradise.

PROSPERO: Sweet now, silence:
    Juno and Ceres whisper seriously,
    There's something else to do: hush, and be mute
    Or else our spell is marr'd.
    Juno and Ceres whisper, and send Iris on employment.

IRIS: You nymphs call'd Naiads of the windring brooks,
With your sedg'd crowns, and ever-harmless looks,
Leave your crisp channels, and on this green land
Answer your summons, Juno does command.
Come temperate nymphs, and help to celebrate
A contract of true love: be not too late.
Enter certain Nymphs.
You sun-burn'd sicklemen of August weary,
Come hither from the furrow, and be merry,
Make holiday: your rye-straw hats put on,
And these fresh nymphs encounter every one
In country footing.

Enter certain Reapers (properly habited): they join with the Nymphs, in a graceful dance, towards the end whereof, Prospero starts suddenly and speaks, after which to a strange hollow and confused noise, they heavily vanish.

PROSPERO: I had forgot that foul conspiracy
Of the beast Caliban, and his confederates
Against my life: the minute of their plot
Is almost come: well done, avoid: no more.
FERDINAND: This is strange: your father's in some passion
That works him strongly.
MIRANDA: Never till this day
Saw I him touch'd with anger, so distemper'd.
PROSPERO: You do look, my son, in a mov'd sort,
As if you were dismay'd: be cheerful sir,
Our revels now are ended: these our actors
(As I foretold you) were all spirits, and
Are melted into air, into thin air,
And like the baseless fabric of this vision
The cloud-capp'd Towers, the gorgeous Palaces,
The solemn Temples, the great Globe itself,
Yea, all which it inherit, shall dissolve,

And like this insubstantial pageant faded
Leave not a rack behind: we are such stuff
As dreams are made on; and our little life
Is rounded with a sleep: sir, I am vex'd,
Bear with my weakness, my old brain is troubled:
Be not disturb'd with my infirmity,
If you be pleas'd, retire into my cell,
And there repose: a turn or two, I'll walk
To still my beating mind.

FERDINAND: MIRANDA: We wish your peace.

Exeunt.

PROSPERO: Come with a thought; I thank thee Ariel: come.

Enter Ariel.

ARIEL: Thy thoughts I cleave to, what's thy pleasure?

PROSPERO: Spirit: we must prepare to meet with Caliban.

ARIEL: Ay my commander, when I presented Ceres
I thought to have told thee of it, but I fear'd
Lest I might anger thee.

PROSPERO: Say again, where didst thou leave these varlets?

ARIEL: I told you sir, they were red-hot with drinking,
So full of valour, that they smote the air
For breathing in their faces: beat the ground
For kissing of their feet; yet always bending
Towards their project: then I beat my tabor,
At which like unback'd colts they prick'd their ears,
Advanc'd their eyelids, lifted up their noses
As they smelt music, so I charm'd their ears
That calf-like, they my lowing follow'd, through
Tooth'd briers, sharp furzes, pricking goss, and thorns,
Which enter'd their frail shins: at last I left them
I' th' filthy-mantled pool beyond your Cell,
There dancing up to th' chins, that the foul lake
O'erstunk their feet.

PROSPERO: This was well done, my bird,
  Thy shape invisible retain thou still:
  The trumpery in my house, go bring it hither
  For stale to catch these thieves.
ARIEL: I go, I go.

Exit.

PROSPERO: A devil, a born devil, on whose nature
  Nurture can never stick: on whom my pains
  Humanely taken, all, all lost, quite lost,
  And, as with age, his body uglier grows,
  So his mind cankers: I will plague them all,
  Even to roaring: come, hang them on this line.

Enter Ariel, loaden with glistering apparel, etc. Enter Caliban,
  Stephano, and Trinculo, all wet.

CALIBAN: Pray you tread softly, that the blind mole may
  not
  Hear a foot fall: we now are near his Cell.
STEPHANO: Monster, your Fairy, which you say is a harm-
  less Fairy, has done little better than play'd the Jack with us.
TRINCULO: Monster, I do smell all horse-piss, at which
  my nose is in great indignation.
STEPHANO: So is mine. Do you hear monster: if I should
  take a displeasure against you: look you.
TRINCULO: Thou wert but a lost monster.
CALIBAN: Good my Lord, give me thy favour still,
  Be patient, for the prize I'll bring thee to
  Shall hoodwink this mischance: therefore speak softly,
  All's hush'd as midnight yet.
TRINCULO: Ay, but to lose our bottles in the pool.
STEPHANO: There is not only disgrace and dishonour in
  that monster, but an infinite loss.
TRINCULO: That's more to me than my wetting: yet
  this is your harmless Fairy, monster.

STEPHANO: I will fetch off my bottle, though I be o'er ears for my labour.

CALIBAN: Prithee, my King, be quiet. See'st thou here
This is the mouth o' th' Cell: no noise, and enter:
Do that good mischief, which may make this Island
Thine own for ever, and I thy Caliban
For aye thy foot-licker.

STEPHANO: Give me thy hand, I do begin to have bloody thoughts.

TRINCULO: O King Stephano, O peer: O worthy Stephano, look what a wardrobe here is for thee.

CALIBAN: Let it alone thou fool, it is but trash.

TRINCULO: Oh, ho, monster: we know what belongs to a frippery. O King Stephano.

STEPHANO: Put off that gown, Trinculo, by this hand I'll have that gown.

TRINCULO: Thy grace shall have it.

CALIBAN: The dropsy drown this fool, what do you mean
To dote thus on such luggage? Let's alone
And do the murther first: if he awake,
From toe to crown he'll fill our skins with pinches,
Make us strange stuff.

STEPHANO: Be you quiet, monster. Mistress line, is not this my jerkin? Now is the jerkin under the line: now jerkin you are like to lose your hair, and prove a bald jerkin.

TRINCULO: Do, do; we steal by line and level, and 't like your grace.

STEPHANO: I thank thee for that jest; here's a garment for 't: wit shall not go unrewarded while I am King of this country: Steal by line and level, is an excellent pass of pate: there's another garment for 't.

TRINCULO: Monster, come put some lime upon your fingers, and away with the rest.

CALIBAN: I will have none on 't: we shall lose our time,
And all be turn'd to barnacles, or to apes
With foreheads villainous low.

STEPHANO: Monster, lay-to your fingers: help to bear
this away, where my hogshead of wine is, or I'll turn
you out of my kingdom: go to, carry this.

TRINCULO: And this.

STEPHANO: Ay, and this.

*A noise of hunters heard. Enter divers Spirits in shape of dogs and
hounds, hunting them about: Prospero and Ariel setting them on.*

PROSPERO: Hey Mountain, hey.

ARIEL: Silver: there it goes, Silver.

PROSPERO: Fury, Fury: there Tyrant, there: hark, hark.
Go, charge my goblins that they grind their joints
With dry convulsions, shorten up their sinews
With aged cramps, and more pinch-spotted make them,
Than pard or cat o' mountain.

ARIEL: Hark, they roar.

PROSPERO: Let them be hunted soundly: at this hour
Lies at my mercy all mine enemies:
Shortly shall all my labours end, and thou
Shalt have the air at freedom: for a little
Follow, and do me service.
　　　　　　　　　　Exeunt.

V. I

Enter Prospero (in his magic robes) and Ariel.

PROSPERO: Now does my project gather to a head:
My charms crack not. My spirits obey, and Time
Goes upright with his carriage: how's the day?

ARIEL: On the sixth hour, at which time, my Lord
You said our work should cease.

PROSPERO: I did say so,
  When first I rais'd the Tempest: say my spirit,
  How fares the King and 's followers?
ARIEL: Confin'd together
  In the same fashion, as you gave in charge,
  Just as you left them; all prisoners sir,
  In the line-grove which weather-fends your Cell,
  They cannot budge till your release: the King,
  His brother, and yours, abide all three distracted,
  And the remainder mourning over them,
  Brimful of sorrow, and dismay: but chiefly
  Him that you term'd sir, the good old Lord Gonzalo,
  His tears run down his beard like winter's drops
  From eaves of reeds: your charm so strongly works 'em
  That if you now beheld them, your affections
  Would become tender.
PROSPERO: Dost thou think so, spirit?
ARIEL: Mine would, sir, were I human.
PROSPERO: And mine shall.
  Hast thou (which art but air) a touch, a feeling
  Of their afflictions, and shall not myself,
  One of their kind, that relish all as sharply,
  Passion as they, be kindlier mov'd than thou art?
  Though with their high wrongs I am struck to th' quick,
  Yet, with my nobler reason, 'gainst my fury
  Do I take part: the rarer action is
  In virtue, than in vengeance: they, being penitent,
  The sole drift of my purpose doth extend
  Not a frown further: go, release them Ariel,
  My charms I'll break, their senses I'll restore,
  And they shall be themselves.
ARIEL: I'll fetch them, sir.
               Exit.

PROSPERO: Ye elves of hills, brooks, standing lakes and
　　groves,
　And ye, that on the sands with printless foot
　Do chase the ebbing Neptune, and do fly him
　When he comes back: you demi-puppets, that
　By moonshine do the green sour ringlets make,
　Whereof the ewe not bites: and you, whose pastime
　Is to make midnight mushrumps, that rejoice
　To hear the solemn curfew, by whose aid
　(Weak masters though ye be) I have bedimm'd
　The noontide Sun, call'd forth the mutinous winds,
　And 'twixt the green sea, and the azur'd vault
　Set roaring war: to the dread rattling thunder
　Have I given fire, and rifted Jove's stout oak
　With his own bolt: the strong-bas'd promontory
　Have I made shake, and by the spurs pluck'd up
　The pine, and cedar.　Graves at my command
　Have wak'd their sleepers, op'd, and let 'em forth
　By my so potent Art. But this rough magic
　I here abjure: and when I have requir'd
　Some heavenly music (which even now I do)
　To work mine end upon their senses, that
　This airy charm is for, I'll break my staff,
　Bury it certain fathoms in the earth,
　And deeper than did ever plummet sound
　I'll drown my book.
　　　　　　　　　Solemn music.
Here enters Ariel before: then Alonso with a frantic gesture,
attended by Gonzalo. Sebastian and Anthonio in like manner
attended by Adrian and Francisco: they all enter the circle which
Prospero had made, and there stand charm'd: which Prospero
observing, speaks:
A solemn air, and the best comforter,

To an unsettled fancy, cure thy brains
(Now useless) boil'd within thy skull: there stand,
For you are spell-stopp'd.
Holy Gonzalo, honourable man,
Mine eyes even sociable to the show of thine
Fall fellowly drops: the charm dissolves apace,
And as the morning steals upon the night
(Melting the darkness) so their rising senses
Begin to chase the ignorant fumes that mantle
Their clearer reason. O good Gonzalo
My true preserver, and a loyal sir,
To him thou follow'st; I will pay thy graces
Home both in word, and deed: most cruelly
Did thou Alonso, use me, and my daughter:
Thy brother was a furtherer in the act,
Thou art pinch'd for 't now Sebastian. Flesh, and blood,
You, brother mine, that entertain'd ambition,
Expell'd remorse, and nature, who, with Sebastian
(Whose inward pinches therefore are most strong)
Would here have kill'd your King: I do forgive thee,
Unnatural though thou art: their understanding
Begins to swell, and the approaching tide
Will shortly fill the reasonable shore
That now lies foul, and muddy: not one of them
That yet looks on me, or would know me: Ariel,
Fetch me the hat, and rapier in my Cell,
I will discase me, and myself present
As I was sometime Milan: quickly spirit,
Thou shalt ere long be free.

> *Ariel sings, and helps to attire him.*
> *Where the bee sucks, there suck I,*
> *In a cowslip's bell, I lie,*
> *There I couch when owls do cry,*

On the bat's back I do fly
After summer merrily.
Merrily, merrily, shall I live now,
Under the blossom that hangs on the bough.

PROSPERO: Why that's my dainty Ariel: I shall miss thee,
But yet thou shalt have freedom: so, so, so.
To the King's ship, invisible as thou art,
There shalt thou find the mariners asleep
Under the hatches: the Master and the Boatswain
Being awake, enforce them to this place;
And presently, I prithee.

ARIEL: I drink the air before me, and return
Or ere your pulse twice beat.

Exit.

GONZALO: All torment, trouble, wonder, and amazement
Inhabits here: some heavenly power guide us
Out of this fearful country.

PROSPERO: Behold Sir King
The wronged Duke of Milan, Prospero:
For more assurance that a living Prince
Does now speak to thee, I embrace thy body,
And to thee, and thy company, I bid
A hearty welcome.

ALONSO: Whe'er thou be'st he or no,
Or some enchanted trifle to abuse me,
(As late I have been) I not know: thy pulse
Beats as of flesh, and blood: and since I saw thee,
Th' affliction of my mind amends, with which
I fear a madness held me: this must crave
(And if this be at all) a most strange story.
Thy Dukedom I resign, and do entreat
Thou pardon me my wrongs: but how should Prospero
Be living, and be here?

PROSPERO: First, noble friend,
　　Let me embrace thine age, whose honour cannot
　　Be measur'd, or confin'd.
GONZALO: Whether this be,
　　Or be not, I'll not swear.
PROSPERO: You do yet taste
　　Some subtlities o' th' Isle, that will not let you
　　Believe things certain: welcome, my friends all.
　　But you, my brace of Lords, were I so minded
　　I here could pluck his Highness' frown upon you
　　And justify you traitors: at this time
　　I will tell no tales.
SEBASTIAN: The Devil speaks in him –
PROSPERO: No:
　　For you, most wicked sir, whom to call brother
　　Would even infect my mouth, I do forgive
　　Thy rankest fault; all of them: and require
　　My Dukedom of thee, which, perforce I know
　　Thou must restore.
ALONSO: If thou be'st Prospero
　　Give us particulars of thy preservation,
　　How thou hast met us here, who three hours since
　　Were wrack'd upon this shore? where I have lost
　　(How sharp the point of this remembrance is)
　　My dear son Ferdinand.
PROSPERO: I am woe for 't, sir.
ALONSO: Irreparable is the loss, and patience
　　Says, it is past her cure.
PROSPERO: I rather think
　　You have not sought her help, of whose soft grace
　　For the like loss, I have her sovereign aid,
　　And rest myself content.
ALONSO: You the like loss?

PROSPERO: As great to me, as late, and supportable
 To make the dear loss, have I means much weaker
 Than you may call to comfort you; for I
 Have lost my daughter.
ALONSO: A daughter?
 O heavens, that they were living both in Naples
 The King and Queen there; that they were, I wish
 Myself were mudded in that oozy bed
 Where my son lies: when did you lose your daughter?
PROSPERO: In this last tempest. I perceive these Lords
 At this encounter do so much admire
 That they devour their reason, and scarce think
 Their eyes do offices of truth: their words
 Are natural breath: but howsoe'er you have
 Been justled from your senses, know for certain
 That I am Prospero, and that very Duke
 Which was thrust forth of Milan, who most strangely
 Upon this shore (where you were wrack'd) was landed
 To be the Lord on 't: no more yet of this,
 For 'tis a Chronicle of day by day,
 Not a relation for a breakfast, nor
 Befitting this first meeting: welcome, sir;
 This Cell's my Court: here have I few attendants,
 And subjects none abroad: pray you look in:
 My Dukedom since you have given me again,
 I will requite you with as good a thing,
 At least bring forth a wonder. to content ye
 As much, as me my Dukedom.
Here Prospero discovers Ferdinand and Miranda,
playing at chess.

MIRANDA: Sweet Lord, you play me false.
FERDINAND: No my dearest love,
 I would not for the world.

MIRANDA: Yes, for a score of Kingdoms, you should
    wrangle,
And I would call it fair play.
ALONSO: If this prove
A vision of the Island, one dear son
Shall I twice lose.
SEBASTIAN: A most high miracle.
FERDINAND: Though the seas threaten they are merciful,
I have curs'd them without cause.
ALONSO: Now all the blessings
Of a glad father, compass thee about:
Arise, and say how thou cam'st here.
MIRANDA: O wonder!
How many goodly creatures are there here!
How beauteous mankind is! O brave new world
That has such people in 't.
PROSPERO: 'Tis new to thee.
ALONSO: What is this maid, with whom thou wast at play?
Your eld'st acquaintance cannot be three hours:
Is she the goddess that hath sever'd us,
And brought us thus together?
FERDINAND: Sir, she is mortal;
But by immortal Providence, she's mine:
I chose her when I could not ask my father
For his advice: nor thought I had one: she
Is daughter to this famous Duke of Milan,
Of whom, so often I have heard renown,
But never saw before: of whom I have
Receiv'd a second life; and second father
This Lady make him to me.
ALONSO: I am hers.
But O, how oddly will it sound, that I
Must ask my child forgiveness?

PROSPERO: There sir stop,
 Let us not burthen our remembrances, with
 A heaviness that's gone.
GONZALO: I have inly wept,
 Or should have spoke ere this: look down you gods
 And on this couple drop a blessed crown;
 For it is you, that have chalk'd forth the way
 Which brought us hither.
ALONSO: I say Amen, Gonzalo.
GONZALO: Was Milan thrust from Milan, that his issue
 Should become Kings of Naples? O rejoice
 Beyond a common joy, and set it down
 With gold on lasting pillars: In one voyage
 Did Claribel her husband find at Tunis,
 And Ferdinand her brother, found a wife,
 Where he himself was lost; Prospero, his Dukedom
 In a poor Isle: and all of us, ourselves,
 When no man was his own.
ALONSO: Give me your hands:
 Let grief and sorrow still embrace his heart,
 That doth not wish you joy.
GONZALO: Be it so, Amen.
Enter Ariel, with the Master and Boatswain amazedly following.
 O look sir, look sir, here is more of us:
 I prophesi'd, if a gallows were on land
 This fellow could not drown: now blasphemy,
 That swear'st grace o'erboard, not an oath on shore,
 Hast thou no mouth by land? What is the news?
BOATSWAIN: The best news is, that we have safely found
 Our King, and company: the next: our ship,
 Which but three glasses since, we gave out split,
 Is tight, and yare, and bravely rigg'd, as when
 We first put out to sea.

ARIEL: Sir, all this service
Have I done since I went.
PROSPERO: My tricksy spirit.
ALONSO: These are not natural events, they strengthen
From strange, to stranger: say, how came you hither?
BOATSWAIN: If I did think, sir, I were well awake,
I 'ld strive to tell you: we were dead of sleep,
And (how we know not) all clapp'd under hatches,
Where, but even now, with strange, and several noises
Of roaring, shrieking, howling, jingling chains,
And mo diversity of sounds, all horrible,
We were awak'd: straightway, at liberty;
Where we, in all her trim, freshly beheld
Our royal, good, and gallant ship: our Master
Capering to eye her: on a trice, so please you,
Even in a dream, were we divided from them,
And were brought moping hither.
ARIEL: Was 't well done?
PROSPERO: Bravely, my diligence; thou shalt be free.
ALONSO: This is as strange a maze, as e'er men trod,
And there is in this business, more than nature
Was ever conduct of: some Oracle
Must rectify our knowledge.
PROSPERO: Sir, my Liege,
Do not infest your mind, with beating on
The strangeness of this business, at pick'd leisure
(Which shall be shortly single) I'll resolve you
(Which to you shall seem probable) of every
These happen'd accidents: till when, be cheerful
And think of each thing well: come hither spirit,
Set Caliban, and his companions free:
Untie the spell: how fares my gracious sir?
There are yet missing of your company

Some few odd lads, that you remember not.
Enter Ariel, driving in Caliban, Stephano, and Trinculo, in
their stolen apparel.

STEPHANO: Every man shift for all the rest, and let no
man take care for himself; for all is but fortune: coragio
bully-monster, coragio.

TRINCULO: If these be true spies which I wear in my head,
here's a goodly sight.

CALIBAN: O Setebos, these be brave spirits indeed:
How fine my master is! I am afraid
He will chastise me.

SEBASTIAN: Ha, ha:
What things are these, my Lord Anthonio?
Will money buy 'em?

ANTHONIO: Very like: one of them
Is a plain fish, and no doubt marketable.

PROSPERO: Mark but the badges of these men, my Lords,
Then say if they be true: this mis-shapen knave;
His mother was a witch, and one so strong
That could control the Moon; make flows, and ebbs,
And deal in her command, without her power:
These three have robb'd me, and this demi-devil;
(For he's a bastard one) had plotted with them
To take my life: two of these fellows, you
Must know, and own, this thing of darkness, I
Acknowledge mine.

CALIBAN: I shall be pinch'd to death.

ALONSO: Is not this Stephano, my drunken butler?

SEBASTIAN: He is drunk now; where had he wine?

ALONSO: And Trinculo is reeling ripe: where should they
Find this grand liquor that hath gilded 'em?
How cam'st thou in this pickle?

TRINCULO: I have been in such a pickle since I saw you

last, that I fear me will never out of my bones: I shall
not fear fly-blowing.

SEBASTIAN: Why how now Stephano?

STEPHANO: O touch me not, I am not Stephano, but a
cramp.

PROSPERO: You 'ld be King o' th' Isle, sirrah?

STEPHANO: I should have been a sore one then.

ALONSO: This is a strange thing as e'er I look'd on.

PROSPERO: He is as disproportion'd in his manners
As in his shape: go sirrah, to my Cell,
Take with you your companions: as you look
To have my pardon, trim it handsomely.

CALIBAN: Ay that I will: and I'll be wise hereafter,
And seek for grace: what a thrice-double ass
Was I to take this drunkard for a god?
And worship this dull fool?

PROSPERO: Go to, away.

ALONSO: Hence, and bestow your luggage where you
found it.

SEBASTIAN: Or stole it rather.

Exeunt Caliban, Stephano, and Trinculo.

PROSPERO: Sir, I invite your Highness, and your train
To my poor Cell: where you shall take your rest
For this one night, which part of it, I'll waste
With such discourse, as I not doubt, shall make it
Go quick away: the story of my life,
And the particular accidents, gone by
Since I came to this Isle: and in the morn
I'll bring you to your ship, and so to Naples,
Where I have hope to see the nuptial
Of these our dear-belov'd, solemniz'd,
And thence retire me to my Milan, where
Every third thought shall be my grave.

ALONSO: I long
   To hear the story of your life; which must
   Take the ear strangely.
PROSPERO: I'll deliver all,
   And promise you calm seas, auspicious gales,
   And sail, so expeditious, that shall catch
   Your royal fleet far off: my Ariel; chick
   That is thy charge: then to the elements
   Be free, and fare thou well: please you draw near.
                  Exeunt Omnes.

EPILOGUE

Spoken by Prospero.

Now my charms are all o'erthrown,
And what strength I have's mine own,
Which is most faint: now 'tis true
I must be here confin'd by you,
Or sent to Naples; let me not
Since I have my Dukedom got,
And pardon'd the deceiver, dwell
In this bare Island, by your spell,
But release me from my bands
With the help of your good hands:
Gentle breath of yours, my sails
Must fill, or else my project fails,
Which was to please: now I want
Spirits to enforce, Art to enchant:
And my ending is despair,
Unless I be reliev'd by prayer
Which pierces so, that it assaults
Mercy itself, and frees all faults.
　As you from crimes would pardon'd be,
　Let your indulgence set me free.

Exit.

NOTES

References are the page and line of this Edition;
the full page contains 33 lines.

P. 22   *The Actors' Names:* This is one of the few lists of characters given in the Folio.

P. 23 L. 17   *Play the men:* act like men.

P. 23 L. 29   *Work the peace of the present:* bring us peace immediately.

P. 24 L. 6   *no drowning mark … gallows:* for 'he that is born to be hanged will never be drowned'; and the boatswain looks like a gallows-bird.

P. 24 L. 27   *Lay her a-hold … off:* 'The ship is on a lee-shore, she has not sea-room, and therein lies the greatest danger. In such circumstances, with the stress of work and anxiety thrown on him by the gale, the boatswain's irritation with the troublesome passengers is most convincing. To ease the ship the top-mast is then struck. This done, they lay the ship to in the fashion then general, that is, by bringing her as near to the wind as she would lie with only the main-course set. This was called "trying", or "lying a-try". A ship thus handled rode easily to the sea, but drove bodily to leeward, away from the wind. If the wind was very severe, a ship could not bear her main-course, and this was now in Shakespeare's mind. The next order, "lay her a-hold", as it stands, is meaningless; there was neither then, nor ever, such a term in use. It is in all probability due to a mishearing on Shakespeare's part. To "lay a ship a-hull" is to bring her as nearly as possible to front the wind and sea and to make her lie in that position with no sail set. In a severe storm this was always done, but of course the ship drove to leeward. It soon appears that if she continues to "hull", the ship must go ashore; the only hope lies in carrying a press of sail in order to claw off the lee-shore, so the boatswain orders the "two

courses", i.e. the equivalent of reefed main and fore-
sails, to be set. This heroic remedy, however, does
not succeed; the ship does not gain sea-room, and
presently strikes. As the event proved, she did not
"split" or go to pieces, as the passengers and crew
feared, but her striking put an end to the boatswain's
work for the present. The whole scene is well thought
out, and, with the single verbal slip of "a-hold",
is technically perfect.' (*Shakespeare's England*, i, 161–2)

our mouths be cold: Here the Boatswain abandons all   P. 24 L. 31
hope and falls to drinking.

wide-chop'd: large-cheeked, because he is drinking   P. 25 L. 5
greedily.

The washing of ten tides: Condemned pirates were   P. 25 L. 7
hanged on the shore at low tide and left until three
high tides had passed over them.

long heath: rough grass.   P. 25 L. 19

furze: a kind of gorse.   P. 25 L. 19

fraughting souls: literally, those who were her freight.   P. 26 L. 6

bootless inquisition: vain questioning.   P. 27 L. 2

liberal Arts: academic learning.   P. 28 L. 16

my state grew stranger: ceased to manage the affairs of   P. 28 L. 19
my state.

Dost thou attend me?: Critics are sometimes troubled   P. 28 L. 21
by Prospero's repeated demand that Miranda shall
listen to his story, as if she were lacking in ordinary
politeness. In fact, the remark is a half-articulate plea
for sympathy. Prospero must now be judged by his
own daughter, and he is desperately anxious that
she shall realize the true causes of his failure as a Duke.

trash for over-topping: 'check for outrunning' – a   P. 28 L. 25
metaphor from training a pack of hounds.

new created: made new creatures by altering their   P. 28 L. 25
minds.

all dedicated To closeness: devoted to private studies.   P. 29 L. 1

O'er-priz'd all popular rate: was worth more than men   P. 29 L. 4
commonly value it.

Absolute Milan: Duke of Milan in fact.   P. 29 L. 22

P. 29 L. 23   *temporal royalties*: kingly power, temporal as opposed to intellectual power.

P. 29 L. 25   *dry … for sway*: thirsty for power.

P. 29 L. 27   *Subject his coronet, to his crown*: i.e. pay homage as to his superior.

P. 30 L. 6   *in lieu o' th' premises*: in return for these conditions.

P. 30 L. 30   *With … ends*: disguised their foul intentions with fair pretexts.

P. 31 L. 13   *undergoing stomach*: courage to endure.

P. 32 L. 9   *zenith*: the highest point, i.e. of my fortunes.

P. 32 L. 24   *to point*: exactly.

P. 32 L. 27   *waist*: that part of the ship that lies between poop and forecastle.

P. 32 L. 28   *flam'd amazement*: appeared in the form of fire – a phenomenon known as St. Elmo's fire.

P. 33 L. 9   *tricks of desperation*: tricks caused by madness.

P. 33 L. 20   *sustaining*: if this is the correct reading it means 'the garments that kept them up'.

P. 33 L. 33   *still-vex'd Bermoothes*: ever stormy Bermudas. See Introduction, p. 16.

P. 34 L. 2   *charm … labour*: my charm added to their weariness.

P. 35 L. 17   *one thing she did*: this good action is not mentioned.

P. 35 L. 20   *blue-ey'd*: with dark rings round the eyes, sunken-eyed.

P. 35 L. 32   *groans … mill-wheels strike*: the clop–clop–clop noise made by a water mill.

P. 37 L. 25   *South-west*: wind from the South was regarded as being unhealthy. Thus Coriolanus curses his soldiers: 'All the contagion of the South light on you.'

P. 38 L. 6   *Water with berries in 't*: Shakespeare seems to have taken this from Strachey's account of the Bermudas adventure (see Introduction, p. 18). He records that the castaways made a pleasant drink with cedar berries.

P. 38 L. 26   *Abhorred slave*: many editors assign this speech to Prospero.

red plague rid: bubonic plague destroy. P. 39 L. 8

old cramps: cramps which come with old age. P. 39 L. 14

aches: pronounced as two syllables, as 'H's'. P. 39 L. 15

Enter ... Ariel, invisible: On the modern stage Ariel P. 39 L. 23
is sometimes an embarrassment, for we are never sure
whether he is supposed to be invisible or not. In
Shakespeare's time there was probably some conventional robe or cloak which denoted invisibility.
Thus in the papers of Philip Henslowe who owned
the Rose Theatre, there is a note that in 1598 he
spent £3 10s. for the Admiral's Men for 'a robe for
to goo invisibell' and 'a gown for Nembia'. (*Henslowe Papers,* ed. W. W. Greg, p. 123). Wordsworth,
in the *Prelude* (Book VII) describes how he visited
various shows in London, including Jack the Giant-
Killer, who donned his coat of darkness, which was
simply labelled with the word 'Invisible' – perhaps
a survival from Elizabethan stage procedure.

It goes on: i.e. Prospero's plan that Miranda shall fall P. 41 L. 8
in love with Ferdinand.

maid, or no: i.e. mortal or goddess. P. 41 L. 17

he does hear me: i.e. 'because by the death of my P. 41 L. 26
father I am now king.'

never since at ebb: i.e. have not ceased flowing. P. 41 L. 28

chang'd eyes: fallen in love; or as John Donne express- P. 42 L. 5
es it in *The Good-morrow:*

My face in thine eye, mine in thine appears,
And plain true hearts do in the faces rest.

My foot my tutor? The head is the tutor to the P. 43 L. 8
body, but Miranda (who is by nature subordinate,
and so 'the foot') is trying to tell her father what to
do.

a laughter: 'The winner is to have the laugh on the P. 45 L. 25
loser, on the principle of the proverb, "He laughs
that wins", Cf. *Othello* IV, 1. 126' (Kittredge).

you're paid: i.e. you've had your laugh as winner. P. 45 L. 29

He ... miss't: i.e. if he starts the first clause with P. 45 L. 33
'though', he is sure to follow up with 'yet'.

P. 46 L. 24   *pockets could speak*: i.e. because the pockets are still wet.

P. 47 L. 1   *widow Dido*: Dido was the Queen of Carthage (the modern Tunis), who entertained Aeneas on his way from Troy to Italy. She was a widow and had vowed eternal fidelity to the memory of her dead husband Acarbas, but she fell in love with Aeneas, who deserted her.

P. 47 L. 11   *miraculous harp*: according to the legends told by Ovid the walls of Thebes came together at the music of Amphion's harp. So, says Anthonio, by like miraculous imagination Gonzalo can create a Carthage at Tunis.

P. 48 L. 19   *loose her to an African*: as 'lose' and 'loose' are both spelt 'loose' in the Folio it is sometimes doubtful which word should be used in a modern text. Here 'loose' is likelier in Sebastian's mouth: it is used of horse and cattle breeding.

P. 48 L. 27   *Which end ... should bow*: whether her dislike or obedience would weigh heavier.

P. 49 L. 11   *plantation*: colonization, but Antonio and Sebastian pretend to take it literally as 'planting'.

P. 49 L. 16   *I' th' Commonwealth ...*: the origin of this passage is given in the Introduction, p. 19. Gonzalo will have perfect communism, without legal agreements (*contracts*), right of inheritance (*succession*), boundaries (*bourn*), rights of private property (*bound of land*).

P. 50 L. 11   *minister occasion*: provide opportunity.

P. 50 L. 23   *bat-fowling*: hunting for birds at night with the aid of a lantern and sticks or bats.

P. 50 L. 25   *adventure my discretion so weakly*: 'I will not lose my reputation for sense so easily by showing anger at such as you'.

P. 50 L. 33   *heavy offer*: chance of deep sleep.

P. 51 L. 18   *occasion speaks thee*: opportunity calls you.

P. 52 L. 2   *if heed me*: if you will listen to me.

P. 52 L. 4   *standing water*: at the turn of the tide when it neither flows nor ebbs.

P. 52 L. 17   *throes ... yield*: is painful to bring forth.

Ten leagues beyond man's life: ten leagues farther   P. 53 L. 7
than a man could travel in a lifetime.

discharge: task to be performed.   P. 53 L. 14

measure us back: retrace her journey after us.   P. 53 L. 21

chough of as deep chat: a cryptic phrase, meaning   P. 53 L. 28
apparently, 'I would become a jackdaw too if I
   talked as much as Gonzalo'.

twenty consciences … candied: Antonio, as a fashion-   P. 54 L. 10
able nobleman, mixes his speech with the allusive
metaphor so popular at the time. He means, 'when
I had my chance of getting Milan from my brother,
I should not have been troubled by twenty consciences; they would have been like sugar, soon melted'

perpetual wink: everlasting sleep.   P. 54 L. 17

They'll hour: 'they'll say it's the right time for   P. 54 L. 21
any dirty business which we suggest.'

Poor-John: dried and salted hake.   P. 57 L. 5

had but this fish painted: had a notice board made   P. 57 L. 9
advertising a freak.

long spoon: because 'he that sups with the Devil   P. 59 L. 14
needs a long spoon'.

constant: steady. Trinculo is pawing Stephano all   P. 59 L. 29
over in his excitement.

pig-nuts: 'earth nut', a plant producing edible tubers.   P. 61 L. 16

scamels: a much-discussed word which does not   P. 61 L. 20
occur anywhere else and is probably therefore a misprint, the likeliest emendation being 'seamew' or
'seamel'=seagull.

Most busy lest: This difficult phrase has been much   P. 62 L. 22
emended by editors 'most busy least'; 'most busy,
least'; 'most busy idlest'; 'most busiless' and many
more. The first involves least change. The general
meaning is 'I am busiest when I cease working and
begin thinking such sweet thoughts'.

Prospero above: I have added *above* for it is obvious   P. 62 L. 23
that Prospero does not enter with Miranda and is
unseen by the lovers. A little later (p. 71 l. 24) he

again looks on from above. The balcony (see illustration, p. 13) was a most convenient part of the Elizabethan stage enabling eavesdroppers to see and hear without being seen.

P. 63 L. 33   *put it to the foil:* bring it into disgrace.

P. 64 L. 7   *features … skillness of:* I have no experience of appearances. 'Feature' meant rather bodily shape than face.

P. 65 L. 26   *who … all:* i.e. every new development is a pleasant surprise to the lovers, but Prospero has foreseen it all.

P. 66 L. 4   *bear up:* crowd on more sail.

P. 66 L. 6   *The folly of this Island:* editors usually print 'Servant-monster! The Folly of this island!' In the Folio ' ?' is often used for ' !'. Our text reproduces the Folio punctuation. The meaning is 'So you call him Servant-monster: what a silly place this Island is, where there are only five people; and three of 'em are reeling drunk'. Trinculo is now hardly coherent.

P. 66 L. 18   *standard:* standard bearer, or ensign, the junior officer in a company; the other two being the captain and the lieutenant. But Caliban is now too unsteady to be a satisfactory 'standard'.

P. 68 L. 2   *pied ninny:* patched fool, because Trinculo, as jester, wears the 'patched', or parti-coloured, dress of his profession.

P. 68 L. 6   *quick freshes:* running springs of fresh water.

P. 68 L. 9   *stock-fish:* dried cod, which was beaten to make it tender.

P. 69 L. 26   *troll the catch:* sing the catch. A catch was a song for three singers, each starting a few words behind the next; a noisy, rowdy affair.

P. 70 L. 4   *picture of Nobody:* i.e. by an invisible player. There is, however, a picture of Nobody in a play printed in 1606 called *No-body and Some-body*. It is all head and no body – like Humpty Dumpty.

P. 70 L. 12   *Be not afeard:* This speech, at first sight, is strangely out of character in the mouth of 'a salvage and deformed slave', and yet it gives a touch of pathos to Caliban.

P. 71 L. 4   *By 'r lakin:* By Our Lady.

maze ... meanders: we have wandered as in a maze   P. 71 L. 5
– this way and that, by straight and winding paths.

Prospero on the top: i.e. on the upper stage. See note   P. 71 L. 24
on p. 62, l. 23.

now I will believe ... there: i.e. he will believe all the   P. 71 L. 31
travellers' yarns. According to the legend there was
only one phoenix. It lived for five hundred years.
Then it built itself a nest of spices, which were set
alight by the rapid beating of its wings. From the
ashes came forth a new phoenix.

Praise in departing: a proverb, implying 'don't give   P. 72 L. 23
thanks for your entertainment until you have seen
how it will end'.

mountaineers, Dew-lapp'd, like bulls ... in their breasts: P. 72 L. 31
Tales of such people were brought home by various
voyagers. Thus Ralegh in the account of his voyage
to Guiana in 1595 wrote: 'Next unto Arui there are
two rivers Atoica and Caora, and on that branch
which is called Caora, are a nation of people, whose
heads appear not above their shoulders; which
though it may be thought a mere fable, yet for mine
own part I am resolved it is true, because every child
in the provinces of Arromaia and Canuri affirm the
same: they are called Ewaipanoma: they are repor-
ted to have their eyes in their shoulders, and their
mouths in the middle of their breasts, and that a
long train of hair groweth backward between their
shoulders. The son of Topiawari, which I brought
with me into England told me that they are the most
mighty men of all the land ... but it was not my
chance to hear of them till I was come away, and if
I had but spoken one word of it while I was there,
I might have brought one of them with me to put
the matter out of doubt. Such a nation was written
of by Mandeville, whose reports were holden for
fables many years, and yet since the East Indies were
discovered, we find his relations true of such things
as heretofore were held incredible: whether it be
true or no, the matter is not great, neither can there
be any profit in the imagination; for mine own part

I saw them not, but I am resolved that so many people did not all combine, or forethink to make the report.' (Hakluyt's *Voyages*, Everyman Edition, vii, 328–9.)

P. 73 L. 2   *putter-out of five for one:* 'The habit of wagering or gambling on difficult and dangerous voyages of exploration, which was laying in a paradoxical fashion the foundations of the insurance system of the country, was a conspicuous sign of the rising tide of reckless speculation.' Gonzalo 'is referring to those merchant voyagers in unknown seas who pledged a sum of money with the capitalist at home on the strange condition that the premium should be forfeited in case nothing further was heard of them, but that five times as much should be paid them on their safe return'. (*Shakespeare's England*, i, 334.)

P. 73 L. 8   *harpy:* a foul creature, half bird of prey, half woman. The episode was suggested by a passage in Virgil's *Aeneid* where the harpies seized and befouled the food of Æneas and his men.

P. 73 L. 11   *hath to instrument this lower world:* Providence which uses the world below as its instrument.

P. 73 L. 12   *never-surfeited:* literally never having eaten to excess. Even the sea, which can retain most things, cannot stomach Alonso and his fellow sinners.

P. 73 L. 22   *dowle that's in my plume:* the Folio reads 'plumb': *dowle*=a downy feather; *plume*=the whole wing.

P. 74 L. 29   *bass my trespass:* proclaim my sin in a deep bass note.

P. 75 L. 25   *halt:* come limping, i.e. she will exceed all praise.

P. 75 L. 27   *Against an oracle:* if even if a god had said the contrary.

P. 76 L. 12   *worser genius:* evil angel, man being supposed to be advised by a good and evil angel. In Marlowe's *Dr. Faustus*, Faustus' Good and Evil Angels are presented as characters striving to influence him.

P. 76 L. 16   *Or ... below:* either that the horses of the Sun have fallen or Night has been imprisoned; i.e. on my wedding day when night seems never to come.

P. 76 L. 28   *Some vanity:* trifling exhibition.

ardour of my liver: heat of my passion. The liver was   P. 77 L. 14
regarded as the seat of passion.

corollary: excess; 'bring too many rather than too   P. 77 L. 16
few'.

Enter Iris: This wedding masque which follows was   P. 77 L. 20
particularly suitable, if not specially written, for the
performance of *The Tempest* at the wedding of Princess Elizabeth. (See Introduction, p. 15). These
symbolical masques were very popular at the Court
of King James, and were often specially composed
for fashionable weddings.

pioned, and twilled brims: a much-disputed phrase   P. 77 L. 25
and variously rewritten by editors. Two interpre-
tations are reasonable. *Pioned* means *dug* (as *pioneer*
=miner), *twilled* may be a form of *twilt*=to pad or
heap up; then the whole phrase means 'banks with
the margins heaped up with the earth freshly dug
out'. The other interpretation is that *pioned*=
covered with peonies (i.e. marsh marigolds or king-
cups) and that *twilled*=*covered with sedge*. But the
truth is that no one knows what either word
means.

pole-clipt: with the poles embraced by vines.   P. 77 L. 30

watery arch: Iris was the messenger of the gods whose   P. 77 L. 33
sign was the rainbow.

dusky Dis: Pluto, god of the underworld, and so   P. 78 L. 20
dark. Pluto seized Ceres' daughter Persephone, and
bore her away to the underworld.

Spring come ... harvest: May spring follow autumn;   P. 79 L. 16
i.e. may there be no bitter winter in your lives
(Kittredge).

windring: winding, perhaps a misprint for 'wandring'   P. 80 L. 1
or 'winding'

rounded with a sleep: Prospero's philosophy is that   P. 81 L. 4
human life is a moment of wakeful dream between
two periods of endless sleep.

presented: represented, took the part of; or else   P. 81 L. 16
'acted as Presenter' (called also the Chorus), who
in many plays introduced the play, as Quince in

A Midsummer Night's Dream presents the players in his company.

P. 82 L. 12   *on this line:* 'line' is probably 'lime-tree', not 'clothes line'; for a little later (p. 85 l. 7) Ariel speaks of the 'line-grove' that weather-fends the Cell.

P. 82 L. 19   *play'd the Jack:* played the knave.

P. 82 L. 27   *hoodwink this mischance:* blindfold this misfortune, i.e. make us forget it.

P. 83 L. 1   *fetch off ... o'er ears:* I will rescue my bottle even if I have to go up to my ears in the pond.

P. 83 L. 10   *O King Stephano, O peer:* Trinculo remembers the well-known and appropriate ballad:

> King Stephen was a worthy peer,
> His breeches cost him but a crown;
> He held them sixpence all too dear,
> Therefore he called the tailor lown.

P. 83 L. 23   *Mistress line ... your grace:* These lines have mystified many editors, but may perhaps be thus explained. Stephano begins by addressing the lime tree as 'Mistress line', as if he were talking to the dealer in an old clothes shop, appealing to her to decide whether the jerkin is his or Trinculo's. Having taken it, he then puns on 'under the line' (i.e. south of the Equator) where the various skin diseases common to long voyages in the tropics caused hair to fall out. Trinculo caps it with a further pun on 'line and level'=on the square. Such passages, after three centuries, fall very flat and have lost all sparkle; but originally, with an audience that saw various meanings in 'jerkin', 'line' and 'loss of hair', a low comedian could have scored.

P. 83 L. 30   *pass of pate:* sally of wit.

P. 84 L. 2   *barnacles:* 'tree-geese'. It was believed, even by such expert botanists as Gerard, that from the barnacles growing on the 'goose tree' emerged small creatures which developed into water-fowl. Gerard concludes his famous *Herbal* with a discourse on these barnacles.

P. 84 L. 16   *aged cramps:* cramp which comes in old age.

Goes upright with his carriage: bears his burden without stooping – because it has now become light.   P. 84 L. 29

weather-fends: protects from the weather.   P. 85 L. 7

demi-puppets: creatures half the size of puppets. Fairies were tiny folk.   P. 86 L. 5

green sour ringlets: the 'fairy rings' seen in English meadows.   P. 86 L. 6

spurs: roots, because the roots of an uprooted tree look like the spurs of a cock's foot.   P. 86 L. 16

pay ... Home: reward your goodness fully.   P. 87 L. 12

reasonable shore: their senses will return soon like the flowing tide and make them reasonable again.   P. 87 L. 23

disease: remove my garments. Prospero is still in his magician's robes and so not recognizable (especially after ten years) to his former associates.   P. 87 L. 27

so, so, so: 'So' used thus, usually indicates action, such as putting on clothes. So Lear (Act III, Scene VI) 'Make no noise, make no noise, draw the curtains: so, so, we'll go to supper i' th' morning.'   P. 88 L. 6

You ... Isle: You still have the taste of the magic nature of the Island.   P. 89 L. 6

Prospero discovers Ferdinand: i.e. he pulls aside the curtain at the back of the stage to reveal the lovers.   P. 90 L. 29

badges: noblemen's servants wore a badge of their masters' coat of arms.   P. 94 L. 17

deal in her command: i.e. take over the Moon's power of controlling the tides.   P. 94 L. 21

EPILOGUE: A concluding epilogue is fairly common in Elizabethan plays, particularly those played at Court. It is usually a conventional apology for the inadequacies of the performance and an appeal for applause. See, for instance, the Epilogue to *A Midsummer Night's Dream*.   P. 97 L. 1

help of your good hands: by your clapping.   P. 97 L. 12

gentle breath: kindly criticism.   P. 97 L. 13

GLOSSARY

admiration: wonder a much stronger word than nowadays.

air: musical air.

allay: abate.

amain: apace.

Argier: Algiers.

aspersion: blessing.

attach'd: literally 'arrested'.

bands: bonds.

basis: base.

bate: (1) abate.
(2) deduct, omit.

bear me: behave myself.

beating: throbbing.

bending: inclining.

blow: make foul.

boiled: boiling, seething.

bombard: a large black leather jug for holding liquor.

boresprit: the Folio spelling of *bowsprit*.

bosky: bushy.

burthen: refrain.

butt: tub.

canker: destroying maggot.

chalk'd: marked out.

chaps: chops.

chirurgeonly: like a good surgeon.

coil: turmoil.

collected: calm.

coragio: courage.

correspondent: responsive, obedient.

course: sail.

court: try to win over.

crabs: crab-apples.

dam: mother.

dearest: most precious.

debosh'd: debauched.

deck: cover over.

distractions: fits of madness.

doit: a small Dutch coin, half a farthing.

drollery: puppet show.

ecstasy: madness.

elements: (1) heavens.
(2) materials.

engine: military machine.

entertained: received.

estate: donate.

event: sequel.

extirpate: root out.

fall: let fall.

fearful: to be feared:

feater: more smartly.

fellow: equal.

few, in: briefly.

filthy-mantled: covered with filthy scum.

flote: flood, sea.
foison: plenty.
fraughting: lit. who were her freight.
frippery: second-hand clothes shop.
furze: a kind of gorse.

gaberdine: cloak.
generation: breed.
gilded: made glow.
glasses: hour-glasses, hours.
glut: swallow greedily.
goss: gorse.
got: begot.

halt: limp.
hests: commands.
hint: occasion.
holp: helped.
Hymen: the god of marriage.

impertinent: irrelevant.
inch meal: by inches, gradually.
injunction: command.
issue: offspring.

Juno: Queen of Heaven.

kibe: blister.

lakin: Little Lady, i.e. the Virgin.
lass-lorn: without his girl.
line-grove: grove of lime trees.

manage: management.

ministers: servants.
miss: do without.
mo: more.
mop: awkward gesture.
mow: grimace.
murrain: plague.

natural: fool.
neat's leather: i.e. shoes.
nerves: sinews.
non-pareil: without an equal.

occupation: trade, manual labour.
out: more than.
owes: owns, possesses.

paragon: perfection.
pard: leopard.
passion (noun): any strong emotion; (*vb.*) suffer emotion.
perdition: loss.
pertly: nimbly.
post: messenger.
presently: immediately.
prime: leading, first.
proper: own.
provision: foresight.

quaint: clever.
quality: kind.

rack: a bank of clouds, so vapour.
rate: estimation.
remember: remind.
remorse: pity.

requit: requited, paid back.

rootedly: fixedly.

salvage: savage.

sanctimonious: religious.

sans: without.

securing: guarding.

set: closed.

siege: excrement.

signiories: lordships.

stale: decay.

steaded: stood in good stead, been useful.

stile: always.

still-closing: ever closing.

stover: grass suitable for fodder.

supplant: displace.

swoln: swollen.

tabor: small drum.

tang: sharp sound.

teen: trouble.

thatched: covered.

throughly: thoroughly.

twink: twinkling.

unback'd: never ridden.

unshrubbed: without shrubs, smooth.

urchins: hedgehogs; also, goblins.

urchin shows: appearances of goblins.

varlets: knaves.

vast: deep night.

visitor: one who visits the sick.

vouched: guaranteed.

ward: posture of defence.

welkin: sky.

wezand: windpipe.

while-ere: just now, erewhile.

whist: silent.

wondered: wonderful.

yare: smart, quick.